A secret to keep

I was an only child, but not exactly. My uncle, Punky, lived with us. This was his thirty-fifth birthday, but he'd always have the mind of a little boy. All my life, he'd been my built-in playmate, more like a younger brother than an uncle....

Of course, I was getting too old to play much anymore. Now, instead of having Punky watch after me, I was watching after him, trying to protect him from outsiders in a world that was growing up and leaving him behind.

Only once, in second grade, had I made the mistake of bringing a girl home with me. Punky had come rushing toward us in his eagerness to play, and the girl had taken one look at his dwarflike body and his child-man face and run screaming from the house in terror.

I'd cried, knowing I could never have a real friend, and I began to think of Punky as a secret I should keep to myself.

OTHER BOOKS YOU MAY ENJOY

The Man Who Loved Clowns

June Rae Wood

PUFFIN BOOKS

For Mom and Dad and my seven
sisters and brothers—but especially
for my brother Richard, the real
"Punky." He was a blessing God
loaned to us for a little while, a
ray of sunshine in our lives.

PUFFIN BOOKS
Published by the Penguin Group
Penguin Young Readers Group, 345 Hudson Street, New York, New York 10014, U.S.A.
Penguin Group (Canada), 10 Alcorn Avenue, Toronto,
Ontario, Canada M4V 3B2 (a division of Pearson Penguin Canada Inc.)
Penguin Books Ltd, 80 Strand, London WC2R 0RL, England
Penguin Ireland, 25 St Stephen's Green, Dublin 2, Ireland (a division of Penguin Books Ltd)
Penguin Group (Australia), 250 Camberwell Road, Camberwell, Victoria 3124,
Australia (a division of Pearson Australia Group Pty Ltd)
Penguin Books India Pvt Ltd, 11 Community Centre,
Panchsheel Park, New Delhi - 110 017, India
Penguin Group (NZ), Cnr Airborne and Rosedale Roads, Albany, Auckland 1310,
New Zealand (a division of Pearson New Zealand Ltd)
Penguin Books (South Africa) (Pty) Ltd, 24 Sturdee Avenue,
Rosebank, Johannesburg 2196, South Africa

Registered Offices: Penguin Books Ltd, 80 Strand, London WC2R 0RL, England

First published in the United States of America by G. P. Putnam's Sons,
a division of The Putnam and Grosset Group, 1992. Reprinted by permission.
First published in paperback by Hyperion Books for Children, 1995
Published by Puffin Books, a division of Penguin Young Readers Group, 2005

20 19 18 17 16 15

Copyright © June Rae Wood, 1992
All rights reserved

THE LIBRARY OF CONGRESS HAS CATALOGED THE PUTNAM EDITION AS FOLLOWS:
Wood, June Rae.
The man who loved clowns / June Rae Wood
p. cm.
Summary: Thirteen-year-old Delrita, whose unhappy life has caused her
to hide from the world, loves her uncle Punky but sometimes feels
ashamed of his behavior because he has Down's syndrome.
ISBN 0-399-21888-2 (hc)
[1. Down's syndrome—Fiction. 2. Mentally handicapped—Fiction. 3. Uncles—Fiction.] I. Title.
PZ7.W84965Man 1992 [Fic]—dc20 91-33861

Puffin ISBN 0-14-240422-5

Printed in the United States of America

Author's Note

This book is a work of fiction. Except for Ronald McDonald, none of the characters exist outside my imagination.

However, the character Punky Holloway was patterned after my brother Richard Olen Haggerman. Richard was born with Down's syndrome on December 17, 1948, in California, Missouri, and died of heart failure at home in Versailles, Missouri, on January 12, 1985.

My parents "let go" of their other offspring as we grew up but they took care of Richard at home for thirty-six years. When my brothers and sisters and I returned to the family farm with children of our own, Richard was there to play with them. Still much like a child himself, he'd build tents for our little ones by throwing old quilts over the clothesline, and he'd line up chairs in the backyard so they could all ride on a make-believe train. In his own simple way he taught yet a third generation about love.

Contents

ONE

The Invisible Girl

"Delrita! Delrita Jensen! Wait up!"

I clutched my books to my chest and plowed on through the sea of sweaty bodies in the junior high hallway. Without looking back, I knew it was that new girl yelling at me. Because she and I had to share a math book, she was the only person in this whole school who didn't consider me invisible. All I wanted was for her to leave me alone.

As I pushed past the mob at Cindi Martin's locker, I concentrated on staying on my feet. Invisible as I was, if I got knocked down I'd be trampled to death.

Although it was September, it felt like mid-July. Most of the kids were wearing summer jams. Not me. If I melted down or got squashed right there by the water fountain, there'd be nothing left but a greasy spot and the blue jeans I had on to hide my pipe-cleaner legs.

"Gotcha," said the new girl, in my ear. She

grabbed the tail of my green T-shirt and hung on—not saying anything, just hanging on like a leech.

I felt my shirt being pulled tight across my chest. If people could see, they'd think I was hiding two Ping-Pong balls inside.

When I finally squeezed past the crowd, the girl let go of my shirt, but she didn't go away.

I glanced sideways at her, wondering how she'd gotten a name like Avanelle Shackleford, a name that was almost bigger than she was.

Her jeans were frayed at the knees, and her shirt was clean but faded and ratty-looking. She was cute, though, if you liked carrot-colored curls and freckles. So why did she want to tag along with me—a tall, skinny brunette who had to stand up twice to cast a shadow?

"Do you do homework on Friday night, or do you wait till the last minute?" Avanelle asked, skipping along to keep up.

"Why?"

"I just wondered when you want the math book."

"Oh. It doesn't matter. You choose."

"I could come over to your house, and we could work together."

"I don't think so," I said, lifting my long brown hair to cool the back of my neck. "I've got things to do."

"Like what?" asked Avanelle. "Maybe I could help you."

Without answering, I walked through the door-

way and onto the sidewalk, away from the noise and
the smell of books and chalk dust. Across the street,
a man was mowing a ditch, and I caught a faint
whiff of dust and dried weeds.

Usually I felt relief when the school day was behind me, but today the cloud didn't lift, because
Avanelle was trying to get chummy. Mom had been
after me to make friends since we'd moved to Tangle
Nook, but I couldn't. Not after that incident with
Georgina Gregory and her bratty little brother, who
lived on our street.

"Like what?" Avanelle repeated. "What do you do
on weekends?"

"Oh, the regular. Chores."

"Your folks make you work all weekend?"

"They don't *make* me work. I do it because I want
to."

Avanelle laughed. "Are you some kind of
weirdo?"

"Don't say that!" I snapped. "I hate that word!"

"Hey, I was just teasing," she replied, edging
away from me.

I was sorry to treat her that way, but I had my
reasons. The next thing I knew she'd start calling me
on the phone or maybe even drop by the house, and
that would be a disaster.

My getaway route was blocked by a dozen buses
parked bumper to bumper. I hoped Avanelle would
climb on a bus. She didn't.

Not knowing what else to say to her, I watched

two boys from our eighth-grade class take down the flag.

Almost in unison, the bus drivers started grinding gears and revving up their engines. The exhaust fumes burned my eyes and throat.

Avanelle coughed and said, "Yuk. Air pollution. That's why we moved from St. Louis."

I stared at her, finding it hard to believe that anybody would trade St. Louis for a dinky little town like Tangle Nook, Missouri.

The buses pulled away, and I hurried across the street, with Avanelle still tailing me.

"Have you always lived in Tangle Nook?" she asked.

"No. We used to live on a farm."

"A real farm with cows and horses?" she asked, wide-eyed.

"No horses, but we had cows and pigs."

"Why did you move to town?"

Not for any reason that I'd dare tell you, I thought, and wished for perhaps the jillionth time that we'd stayed on the farm. Life would be a whole lot easier if we didn't have close neighbors.

I hadn't answered her question, but maybe Avanelle hadn't noticed. Sighing, she said, "We once had a pet chicken named Henrietta."

"You had a chicken in the city?"

"Not for long. She got stolen."

We walked in silence for a couple of minutes, until Avanelle said, "I just turned thirteen. How old are you?"

Was she overly friendly, or was she just determined to pry information out of me one way or another? I kicked at a stone before answering, "I'm thirteen, too."

"Good," she said, and giggled as if I'd told her she'd won the lottery.

I couldn't see where being thirteen was all that funny. Even my mom said it was an awkward age—too old for toys and too young for boys.

"What about the math book?" asked Avanelle. "Do you want to take it, or should I?"

"You take it. Just tell me where you live, and I'll come and get it when I need it."

"I live on Magnolia behind McDonald's, but I'd be glad to bring—"

"I *said* I'd come and get it!"

I saw the hurt in Avanelle's emerald eyes, but that was better than the goggle-eyed stare that would replace it if she ever showed up at my house.

"Here's where I turn off. I hope you're in a better mood when you come to get the math book," said Avanelle, leaving me at the corner.

It occurred to me that if her house was behind McDonald's, she'd gone several blocks in the wrong direction just to walk with me. Well, that was her idea, not mine. I shrugged, glad to be invisible again.

TWO

Out of the Frying Pan, Into the Fire

I was an only child, but not exactly. My uncle, Punky, lived with us. This was his thirty-fifth birthday, but he'd always have the mind of a little boy. All my life, he'd been my built-in playmate, more like a younger brother than an uncle.

My earliest memory was of him hauling me into the house under one arm and saying, "Poop pants," as he plunked me down at Mom's feet. I could picture him throwing quilts over the clothesline to make a tent for us and lining up chairs in the backyard to make a train. Of course, I was getting too old to play much anymore. Now, instead of having Punky watch after me, I was watching after him, trying to protect him from outsiders in a world that was growing up and leaving him behind.

Only once, in second grade, had I made the mistake of bringing a girl home with me. Punky had come rushing toward us in his eagerness to play, and the girl had taken one look at his dwarflike body and his child-man face and run screaming from the house in terror.

I'd cried, knowing I could never have a real friend, and I began to think of Punky as a secret I should keep to myself.

But not everybody was afraid of Punky. Some people called him names, like "dummy" and "weirdo." Others just laughed. Happy-go-lucky Punky never knew when people were making fun of him. If he saw someone laughing, he thought they were happy, too, and he laughed with them.

At the farm I hadn't had to worry about other kids' reactions to Punky. I'd had a couple of friends at my old school, but that's where I'd kept them—at school.

Sometimes, lying awake at night, I'd hear my parents discussing me. Dad thought I was a natural loner, like him. Mom thought I needed to be in town, close to other kids my age. About a year ago, she started trying to convince Dad to leave the farm and open an antique shop in Tangle Nook.

In May, we made the big move. I was scared about leaving my old life behind and starting over in a new place. To chase away my fears, I'd think about the tree I'd once seen growing from a rock. Maybe I'd be like that tree, which stood proud and willowy after fighting its way to the sun, while the rock was cracked with a deep, jagged scar all the way to the ground.

I never did burst through the rock, and on the

very first day in Tangle Nook, I knew I'd jumped out of the frying pan into the fire.

It happened about four months ago, but I can see it now, plain as yesterday. Punky kept peeking into the moving van, watching for his swing set. "My swing?" he'd say every time Dad and the workmen hauled out a piece of furniture.

"Soon, Punky," Dad would promise as he heaved and grunted under the weight of Mom's highboy or china cabinet or solid oak table.

At last the swing set was unloaded, and a mover helped Dad carry it to the backyard. Punky, wearing his cowboy hat and a red jogging suit and carrying the stick that was his pretend microphone, followed close behind.

Dad set the poles and hung the chains, and the minute the seats were in place, Punky announced, "My swing." He started swinging and singing into his microphone about Jesus and Santa Claus and a sunshiny day.

When Dad went back to work, I sat in the other swing. I soon realized, though, that I wasn't the only person in the audience. Someone was hiding and giggling behind the shrubs. Scooting off the swing, I told Punky I'd be back in a minute.

"Yeah, D.J. Pretty girl, D.J.," he sang, using the nickname he'd given me because he couldn't say "Delrita."

I ran in the back door and out the front, and managed to slip up behind the intruders. A girl about my age and a boy about seven were crouched low behind the spirea bushes, their hands clamped over their mouths to quiet their snickering.

"Who are you?" I demanded. "What do you want?"

They jumped and whirled around to face me. The girl gave me a canary-eating grin and said, "We're the Gregorys. We—uh—just wanted to see our new neighbors."

"Did you have to sneak around in the bushes to do it?"

"We—he—that fellow is different," she stammered, pushing her long blond hair back behind her ears.

Revelation. Columbus discovering America. But I didn't want to start off on the wrong foot, so I swallowed the hateful words I was thinking and tried to smile as I said, "So Punky doesn't look and act like the average person. What is average, anyway?"

The girl didn't answer, because Punky came around the shrubbery, saying, "Hi, pretty girl," and patted her on the shoulder. She pulled away as if she'd been burned, eyeing Punky and his microphone stick fearfully.

It made me furious that she thought Punky was funny at a distance but scary up close, and I said, "He doesn't bite."

Punky, meanwhile, wanted someone to speak to him. He pointed to his swing set and said, "My swing." It was an invitation to the kids to join him there, but they didn't move. If they had, their bulging eyeballs would have popped right out of their heads.

I waited, giving the Gregorys a chance to say something nice to Punky, but all they did was stare. The boy's blond hair was cut short and spiked on the top, and the two cowlicks at his freckled forehead gave him a devilish look.

"Come on, Punky," I said finally, grabbing his arm and pulling him toward the house.

But Punky didn't want to go inside. He wanted to swing. I couldn't leave him there alone to be laughed at, so I turned my back on the Gregorys and started swinging, too. After a while, I looked and they were gone, but I couldn't shake the feeling that they were somewhere close by—watching, watching.

My second day in town was worse. When I enrolled at Tangle Nook Junior High, that Gregory girl was working in the office.

"Georgina," said the counselor when she'd finished making out my schedule, "Delrita's in your class. Before the bell rings, will you show her where to find the seventh-grade lockers?"

"Sure, Mrs. Romano," Georgina replied sweetly, as if she'd never seen me before. She didn't speak to me when she led me down the hall, but I saw all the grins and nods that passed between her and the other students. I figured Georgina had kept the phone lines hot, getting the word out overnight. Later, I found a crumpled, dirty note lying in the hall. I picked it up and fought back tears as I read: "Steer clear of the new girl. Georgina says she's got a weird relative, and she's probably weird, too."

The other kids ignored me, and that hurt more than I cared to admit. Before long, I'd decided they had nothing on me. I could play their game. I could be happy being invisible. Besides, not having any friends in my new school was a hundred times better than dealing with my burning sense of guilt—guilt that I loved Punky with all my heart and yet felt ashamed of him for the first time in my life.

THREE

The Birthday Boy

As I watched Avanelle walk away from me, I felt terrible about being so unfriendly. She probably thought I was like the other kids, who hadn't exactly beaten a path to her locker when she enrolled in school this morning. Avanelle didn't know yet about my being invisible, but it was just a matter of time before someone would tell her or pass her a note. I wasn't going to set myself up to be hurt again.

We shared the same lunch period and the same math book, and we had three classes together in a row—art, PE, and math. Whether I liked it or not, we'd been thrown together.

Georgina Gregory had PE class with us, too. If she passed the word during fourth hour Monday, Avanelle would be out of my hair. If she didn't, Avanelle would probably tag along after me again after school. What if she just kept walking and talking all the way to my house and then expected me to invite her in for a Coke?

As I turned onto Mulberry Lane, Georgina's bratty little brother cried, "Watch out!" as he grazed past me on a bicycle and wheeled into his yard. He was laughing because I'd jumped about two feet straight up.

"Hey, boy," I yelled, "don't you know it's against the law to ride on the sidewalk?"

"So? Whatcha gonna do about it?" he yelled back before ducking in his front door.

You and your sister make a good pair, I fumed. You're brave from a distance, but cowards up close. Remembering how Georgina had shied away from Punky's touch, I clenched my fists and stormed past the house.

I knew Punky didn't look normal, but he didn't look scary, either. He just looked like anybody else who had Down's syndrome—moon-faced, with almond-shaped eyes, doughy white skin, and a thick tongue that seemed too big for his mouth.

I could feel the Gregory boy's eyes watching me, and I imagined I heard him laughing. The brat. You couldn't expect much from a kid who brought his friends over to spy on Punky whenever he got the chance.

When I was almost home, I made a conscious effort to wipe the frown off my face and relax. I didn't want to spoil Punky's birthday.

As I opened the screen door, he said, "Hi, pretty girl," and got up stiffly from his cross-legged position in front of the television. Since it was so hard for him to get up and down, I don't know why he wanted to sit on the floor. But that's where he always sat, at a table with sawed-off legs that he pushed up against the TV.

Punky grinned and hitched up the elastic waistband of his red britches. He was so short and roly-poly, jogging pants were the only kind that fit.

I tossed my books on the couch and gave him a hug. "Hi, birthday boy. What's for supper?" I asked, as if I didn't know.

"Fried chinny."

I smiled. Mom would have fried a chicken every night for Punky, but to keep Dad happy she kept it down to every other day.

"Cake, presents, party tonight," said Punky, clapping his stubby hands. Each of his fingers had a bump on the first knuckle, from being chewed.

"Presents!" I teased. "What makes you think you'll get presents?"

"Shirley said," he replied matter-of-factly, taking my hand and pulling me into the kitchen, where Mom was drawing an icing clown on his birthday cake.

Mom stopped squeezing the red frosting from the tube for a moment and rubbed her wrist. She always wore black slacks because they were slenderizing, but I wished she'd get rid of that shirt. Its wide horizontal stripes made her look twenty pounds heavier.

"Hi, hon. How was school today?" she asked.

I didn't tell her that I was the only student in sixth hour who didn't rate a partner for science lab, or that Mrs. Wiseman had called on everyone to read parts of *Evangeline* except me. What I said was,

"Nothing to shout about. I got a B on my book report, and Mr. Casey thinks I have artistic promise."

"Promise? That's an understatement if I ever heard one."

"You're pretty artistic yourself," I said as I admired the clown taking shape on the cake.

"My clown . . . my birthday . . . my chinny," said Punky, pointing first to the cake, then to himself, and then lifting two bags of chicken that were thawing in the sink.

"Two chickens, Mom?" I said.

"I'm afraid so. Your Uncle Bert and Aunt Queenie are coming for supper."

"But why?" I asked, trying not to whine. Aunt Queenie's real name was Queen Esther, after a famous queen in the Bible, so she thought she was royalty.

"Party," said Punky.

"Because I invited them," replied Mom, adding the final touches to the clown. "Now that we live so close, it's only right."

"But Aunt Queenie—"

"Delrita, she's my brother's wife. We can't change that."

"She'll spend the whole evening complaining about the way you take care of Punky."

"I'm a big girl. I can take it. . . . Who wants to lick the bowl?"

"I do," Punky and I chimed together. He took the bowl, I got some spoons, and we went to the sawed-off table to watch commercials on TV. Punky loved commercials, and he was always flipping the channels back and forth, watching for his favorites. Our cupboards overflowed with boxes of detergents that danced, toilet paper that unrolled itself, and several kinds of cat food, even though we'd never owned a cat.

Aunt Queenie said we were spoiling Punky, and I had to admit she was right, although we had a good reason. Doctors had warned us that he wouldn't live very long, because he had a bad heart.

The frosting was too sweet for me on an empty stomach. My vision was blurred, too, from sitting so close to the TV. I got up to move to the couch and surrendered the bowl to Punky, who scraped at it with his spoon and his fingers to clean up every bit. When he was finished, his round face was sticky with red icing.

"Better wash up," I said.

"Wait a minute."

With Punky, a minute could be a minute or an hour and a half. He didn't budge, but sat there twisting his wiry brown hair with his left hand and changing the channel with his right.

I grinned, thinking about my dad's complaint that the only things he ever got to watch on TV were the advertisements for soap.

"Look, D.J.," Punky said happily. "Clown."

From where I sat, I couldn't see much except the back of Punky's head, including the bald spot where he had twisted his hair out. When I leaned over and saw a kids' program featuring Jellybean the Clown, I knew Punky wouldn't touch the dial again until the show was over. Now would be a good time to wrap his birthday present.

Green was my favorite color, as anybody with one eye could tell the moment he stepped into my room with its forest-green carpet and mint-colored walls. The sea-green princess curtains matched the spread on my four-poster bed.

Nearly everything in my closet was green, too, and Mom said my wardrobe looked like leftovers from a St. Patrick's Day parade.

I pulled out my old Barbie doll suitcase, which held the present I'd carved for Punky. I'd gotten rid of the dolls ages before, but the case was perfect for my woodcarving tools. It was funny how I'd never had the patience to dress Barbie in those teeny-tiny clothes, and yet I could whittle on a block of wood for hours.

When I opened the compartment where my basswood carvings were stored, staring up at me was my first project, an ugly blob of a snowman. I'd saved it as a reminder of how much I'd learned—and how much I still didn't know—about woodcarving.

I passed over the snowman and picked up the little clown I had carved and painted for Punky. His smile was slightly crooked, but he definitely looked like Jellybean, with his yellow hair, orange jumpsuit, and gaudy purple shoes.

Jellybean was only four inches high, so he fit perfectly in a big matchbox. I wrapped the package, then hid it at my side as I carried it down the hall.

Punky was enjoying the program on TV, and I smiled on my way to the kitchen. His giggles reminded me of doves cooing in a barnloft.

The smell of chicken frying, fresh cucumbers, and green onions made me realize I was starving. The cooks at school had served cardboard pizza for lunch.

"Want me to set the table?" I asked, to hurry things along.

"Sure," Mom said, "but use the antique dishes and the good silverware." Her face was pink from the heat of the stove, and her dark hair curled in little ringlets at the back of her neck. Lucky Mom. When *my* hair got damp, it hung limp as a dead cat.

I counted out five plates from the china cabinet but went to the cupboard for Punky's. He wouldn't eat unless his food was served on a red plastic plate.

When I heard Dad's car pull into the carport, I knew it was exactly twelve minutes after five. You could set the clock by my father, who closed our antique shop promptly at five o'clock, then dropped by the bank with his day's deposit and drove home in twelve minutes flat.

"Hi, squirt," he said to me as he came in the back door. Glancing at the table, he said to Mom, "I see Bert and Queenie accepted the invitation. I hope you've got your armor. Now that her majesty has done a few hours' volunteer work with the handicapped, she thinks she's the expert."

"Shhhh," said Mom. "They'll be here anytime."

Dad winked at me and ran a hand across his sandy hair. He made his tall, thin body ramrod straight and put his hands on his hips. "I declare, Shirley," he said, mocking Aunt Queenie as he pranced around the table, "you're going to kill us all with your fried food. Why, I can feel my arteries slamming shut this minute."

"Oh, Sam," said Mom, giggling and shooing him away to the shower.

I heard car doors closing. My aunt and uncle had arrived. Instead of coming in the back door, which was closer, they went around to the front and rang the bell.

"Would you get that, Delrita," Mom asked, "while I run a comb through my hair?"

I headed for the living room and realized, too late, that Punky hadn't budged from in front of the TV. He was staring spellbound at a toothpaste commercial. "Punky! Hurry! Wash your face," I said.

"Wait a minute," he replied, not taking his eyes off the set.

I hesitated, willing the commercial to end. As I glanced out the screen door, I decided there was a shade of green I didn't like. Uncle Bert was wearing hideous green pants and a bright yellow shirt with a brown tie. The clothes, and the blond toupee bushing out from beneath his brown golf hat, made him look like a giant sunflower.

"Hurry up, Delrita. It's hot out here," said Aunt Queenie. Even though she could see me, she would never push the door open and walk right in. She stood there tapping her foot impatiently as if the bun she wore like a crown would melt and slide off onto the porch.

The commercials went on and on, until finally I had to open the door or have a good reason not to.

"I declare, Delrita," said my aunt, pushing past me into the living room, "you're as slow as Christmas."

"Christmas! Santy Claus!" cried Punky, getting up at last with a wide grin on his sticky face.

"Punk-Man," boomed Uncle Bert, stooping to give Punky a one-armed bear hug since his other arm was clutching a present. He didn't seem to mind that Punky was kissing his cheek, icing and all.

Punky patted the gift and looked at me. "See, D.J.? Presents. Shirley said."

When it was Aunt Queenie's turn for a kiss, she backed away, saying, "This is a new dress. I'll wait until you've washed your face."

FOUR

Aunt Queenie

With a clean red T-shirt and a freshly scrubbed face, Punky made a beeline for Aunt Queenie. As he stood on tiptoes to kiss her cheek, Uncle Bert said playfully, "Whoa, Punk-Man, that's my girl."

"My girl," argued Punky.

"No, she's my girl."

Punky folded his arms across his chest and said, "She's my girl, you old goat."

Uncle Bert roared with laughter, and even Aunt Queenie smiled.

While Mom and I were setting supper on the table, Dad and Uncle Bert talked about my uncle's real estate business. Punky was telling Aunt Queenie about the clown on TV, but she either didn't understand what he was saying or didn't want to. She kept saying, "Slow down, Punky. I know you can speak more clearly if you take it slow."

Dad asked the blessing, and as soon as he said,

"Amen," Punky said, "Bang!" This was Punky's signal that all was right with his world, but Aunt Queenie frowned her disapproval.

"Horns," said Punky, pointing to the chicken wings on the platter.

"Yes, Punky, they're all yours," said Mom, dishing up the four wings onto his plate and adding green beans, salad, and mashed potatoes and gravy.

"Hey, Punk-Man," said Uncle Bert, "leave some for me."

"You're a fat boy," replied Punky, getting up from the table and carrying his meal to the living room.

"I declare, Shirley. I don't know how you can let Punky just do as he pleases, eating all over the house," said Aunt Queenie.

Dad and I exchanged secret smiles. Wouldn't she hit the ceiling if she knew that as soon as Punky cleaned the meat off a horn, he'd fling the bone behind the TV?

"There's such a thing as good manners," my aunt went on, "and it doesn't look right for him not to eat with the family."

"Queenie," said Mom, quietly but firmly, "did you ever think that Punky is with the family twenty-four hours a day, and maybe he likes having a few minutes to himself?"

"You've spoiled him. No, I take that back. Your mother spoiled him, and you're just making it worse."

"Maybe so, but he has so few pleasures in life,

why shouldn't he get to do what makes him happy?"

"But he's never even been to school," argued Aunt Queenie. "You've had him since he was sixteen, and you could have sent him until he was twenty-one."

Uncle Bert looked uncomfortable. He wiped his face with his napkin and said uneasily, "Queenie, we've been through all this before. You know Mama took Punky to be tested once when he was a little boy, and she came home angry and humiliated because the testing wasn't fair."

Aunt Queenie glared at Uncle Bert as if to ask, Just whose side are you on?

"That's right," said Mom. "The school gave him a standard IQ test for twelve-year-olds, and he failed miserably. One of the questions was 'How do you describe the handle of a knife?' I'm thirty-seven years old, reasonably intelligent, and I'm not sure *I* could describe the handle of a knife well enough to pass an IQ test!"

Aunt Queenie drew a deep breath and looked heavenward, probably praying for patience. "Things have changed since Punky was a little boy. Nowadays they have special schools and Special Olympics. There are sheltered workshops where the handicapped can work under supervision. Now that you live so close, Punky could get a job at the workshop here in town."

"You would actually have me send Punky to that old warehouse?" Mom asked in disbelief. "It's dark and depressing, with not a window in the place! What's more, it's full of strangers who are worse off than he is!"

"Punky needs something to do," insisted Aunt Queenie. "Just look at how he chews his fingers and twists the hair right out of his head."

Mom was trying hard to keep her temper. "Queenie," she said, "before Mama died, I gave her my word that I'd keep him with me always, and that's what I'm doing. I know you've helped some with the handicapped, but you haven't lived it. Mama and I have, and Bert. Ask *him* what it's like to see people poking fun and making mean comments about someone you love."

Uncle Bert, who'd been taking a drink of iced tea, started choking. I wondered if it was on purpose. After all, he had to live with Aunt Queenie.

My aunt, glancing from Uncle Bert back to Mom, drummed her manicured fingers on the table and said, "I know you want what's best for Punky. The workshop—"

"No," said Mom, her blue eyes smoldering.

"Well, I declare," began Aunt Queenie, and I was afraid I'd scream if she declared anything one more time.

"Declare all you want," replied Mom, "but I'm Punky's guardian, and what I say goes."

That was probably the longest meal of my life. There wasn't much to talk about after Mom closed the subject of Punky. We all just sat there chewing and swallowing.

Aunt Queenie's feelings were hurt, but at least that meant she wouldn't be asking me a lot of questions. Since she didn't have kids of her own, I don't know why she always seemed so interested in me, my school, and my friends. Especially now, being invisible, I was a real nobody.

When the dishes were cleared away, Mom set out the packages.

I lit the candles on the clown cake, feeling sad at the number thirty-five. According to the doctor, it was rare for people with Down's syndrome to live past forty.

"Don't forget the matches," said Mom.

I nodded and hid them in a drawer. Once, Punky had lit a candle to look for something under the bed and had forgotten to blow it out.

"Birthday cake and presents," Mom called into the living room.

Usually you needed a stopwatch to see if Punky was moving, but this time it took him about three seconds to reach the kitchen.

When he tore into Uncle Bert's package and found a portable radio, he said, "Wait a minute," and headed off with it to his bedroom. In a moment he was back, singing into his stick microphone.

The next present was from Mom and Dad—a T-shirt that said "Surf Bum" and a pair of red socks. Immediately Punky kicked off his shoes and started ripping off his old shirt.

"Well, I declare, Punky," said Aunt Queenie.

"Are you going to strip down right here in the kitchen?"

"Yup," Punky grunted as he pulled on the new shirt.

Uncle Bert patted his round belly and said, "You're a fat boy."

"*You're* a fat boy, you old goat."

The last two gifts from Mom and Dad were a box of crayons and a cordless microphone.

"You won't need that old stick anymore," said Dad. "This is the real thing." Speaking into the new microphone, he said, "Happy birthday."

Punky looked startled at the magnified sound. He grabbed the mike from Dad, crammed it back into the box, and shoved it at Uncle Bert. "You have it," he said.

"But Punky," said Dad, "you can sing with it in the backyard."

"Don't want it. Bert have it," replied Punky, and that was that.

I had saved my present for last. When Punky saw the little clown, he said, "Jellybean!" and planted a kiss on my forehead.

"Delrita, that's beautiful," exclaimed Aunt Queenie. "The last I knew, you were hacking away at a pitiful little lump of a snowman."

"That was two years ago. I've learned a lot since then."

"Well, I'm impressed. What other things have you carved?"

"Oh, I don't know," I murmured, watching

Punky as he disappeared again down the hall.

"She made these for me," said Mom, opening the curved glass doors of her china cabinet and removing a girl, a boy, and a dog that I'd stained with an oak-tinted varnish. The creases and folds had stained darker than the bodies, so the pieces looked antique.

Aunt Queenie got up and studied each carving under the light. Smiling at me, she asked, "Have you ever thought about selling some of your work at a craft show?"

"Oh, no," I said hastily. "My stuff isn't good enough."

"It certainly is. These pieces remind me of the ones I've seen at Silver Dollar City."

"Thanks," I said, glowing at the compliment. The carvings at Silver Dollar City were the work of a master, and I secretly longed to be as skillful as he was.

Punky came back with his metal Jellybean lunch box, where he carried his daily stash of treasures. Today the box held five of my painted carvings. "Clowns," he said. He lined them up on the table next to Jellybean and counted, "One, two, three, four, five."

"Hey, Punk-Man, I'll take this one," said Uncle Bert, pretending to pick out a clown for himself.

"Okay. You have it," said Punky, but he was quick to remove the rest from his brother's reach.

Uncle Bert chuckled and gave him back the clown. "Just testing you, Punk-Man, to see if I should give you this." Reaching into his pocket, he said, "I've got a coupon book for one Richard Punk-Man Holloway. It's worth five dollars at Mc-Donald's."

"Big Mac! All ri-i-ght!" cried Punky. He went behind Uncle Bert, lifted his toupee, and kissed him on the top of his bald head.

After my aunt and uncle had left and my parents had gone to bed, I stayed up late with Punky. I liked spending Friday nights carving and watching commercials on TV, so why, all of a sudden, was I wondering how many girls had showed up for Cindi Martin's slumber party?

I threw an old sheet over the couch to catch the worst of my wood shavings and sat down to work on a trumpeter swan. I used a tool called a veiner to shape the swan's body. The head and neck were still just a hunk of wood, and I wouldn't try carving them tonight. Maybe tomorrow, when I felt fresh and rested. I'd carved other kinds of animals without much trouble, but somehow my swans always ended up with broken necks. Punky already had three of them that could pass for deformed ducks.

Punky's hands were busy, too. When he wasn't flicking the channel selector, he was peeling the paper off his new crayons and breaking them into tiny pieces of exactly the same size. Beside him on the floor was a peck basket full of the crayons he had accumulated over the years—hundreds, maybe thousands of them, all peeled and broken. To Punky,

they were treasures to be rolled back and forth end-
lessly on his sawed-off table.

Around midnight, when I heard the first TV station signing off the air, I brushed the wood shavings
off my lap and got up.

"Flag, D.J.," said Punky as he scrambled to his
feet. He wouldn't allow anybody to sit through
"The Star-Spangled Banner," even if it was just on
TV. He snapped a soldier's salute and held it for a
full minute as the Stars and Stripes waved across the
screen.

Twice more we went through the ritual as the
other two stations ended their programming for the
night. When the last notes of the last national an-
them faded away, Punky stretched and yawned.

"Ready for bed, birthday boy?" I asked.

"Yup," he said, switching off the television.

I glanced around the living room before turning
off the light. Except for the antique love seat and the
marble-top table with its pineapple-lace doily, every
stick of furniture was cluttered with Punky's and my
belongings.

The carpet, littered with wood shavings and
crayon papers, looked like the bottom of a hamster
cage. I grinned. Aunt Queenie would declare herself
into a snit if she knew about the pile of horn bones
behind the TV.

FIVE

The Bratty Gregory Kid

"Delrita," said Mom, shaking me awake, "I need to talk to you."

"Mmmnnnggghh," I grunted from the midst of my dream.

"Come on, get up, sleepyhead."

I rolled out from under the covers and sat like a zombie on the edge of the bed. "Will you carry my eyes downstairs?" I mumbled. "I can't see the steps in the morning."

Mom laughed. It was the same silly question I'd asked her when I was four years old and we lived in Grandma's old farmhouse. "Come on," she said, "and I'll fix you a cup of hot chocolate."

In the kitchen, Dad was seated at the table. He was dressed for an auction, in khaki pants and a pullover shirt with a notepad sticking out of the pocket. "Good morning, squirt," he said over his coffee cup.

Reaching for a slice of leftover bacon as I collapsed into a chair, I said sleepily, "Hi. What's up?"

"Your mother wants to go to an estate auction with me today, if you think you and Punky will be okay here by yourselves."

"Sure."

Mom handed me a cup of hot chocolate that was mushy with marshmallows, and said, "They've advertised a roll-top desk that I'd like to look at."

I nodded.

"Are you sure you and Punky will be all right? The sale is way down at Versailles, and we wouldn't be within hollering distance if you had any trouble."

By "trouble," she meant the possibility that Punky would have another spell with his heart. None of us liked to talk about it, but it was always there—the worry that Punky might die.

"There won't be any trouble," said Dad. "Punky hasn't been sick for almost a year. Besides, Delrita knows how to use the nitroglycerin pills, and the numbers of the doctor, the hospital, and the ambulance are right there by the phone."

"Yeah, Mom, I know I'm supposed to put the pills under Punky's tongue. And I can call for help if I need it."

"All right," she said slowly. "I really would like to get out of the house for a while. . . . Sam, should we tell her about next weekend or save it as a surprise?"

"Tell me," I said, wide awake. "Don't save it."

"There's a big estate auction," said Dad, "and

there'll be antique buyers from all over Missouri."

"But what's the surprise?"

"It's at Branson."

"Branson?" I cried. "Does that mean we're going to Silver Dollar City?"

Dad chuckled. "If you and Punky can stand to look at old furniture with Shirley and me, I reckon we can put up with a pioneer town full of hillbillies and old-fashioned rides."

I pulled on my softest, most faded pair of jeans and my favorite knock-around T-shirt, then stood before the mirror of my heavy oak dresser.

The mirror was antique, and it reflected a wavy image back at me. As I brushed my hair, I thought how I looked like the little wooden urchin that had caught my eye in the window of the woodcarving shop at Silver Dollar City. She had a heart-shaped face with a flat nose and almost no chin, and her eyes were big and blue as a summer sky.

I had pulled Punky into the shop that day, thinking I would choose the urchin as my souvenir. The price was way beyond what I could afford, but when we turned to go, I spied the master woodcarver at work. As I watched him create a trumpeter swan in flight, my own hands itched to shape something beautiful from a block of wood.

Later that afternoon, when we met my parents at the Old Mine Restaurant, Punky was sporting a black cowboy hat with a silver band, and I was clutching my first woodcarving tool in a crumpled sack.

My folks at first thought I'd wasted my money. They couldn't understand why I would buy a cheap pocketknife and a six-inch chunk of basswood when the shops were overflowing with souvenirs more suitable for an eleven-year-old girl.

My first carving was that awful snowman. Besides not knowing how or where to start, I lacked patience and I kept cutting my fingers. I was on the verge of giving up woodcarving forever when, on my twelfth birthday, Mom and Dad gave me a set of tools and a woodcarving book for beginners.

What a difference it made when I had the proper tools, and guidelines to follow. Now I drew my designs on cardboard, transferred them to the basswood, and had Dad cut the basic outlines with his band saw.

I smiled as I fastened my hair in a ponytail. Dad was into carpentry, not woodcarving, but he was my biggest fan.

In the living room, the morning breeze was blowing through the window, scattering leftover wood shavings like dandruff on the couch and carpet. Wishing for luck, I opened the Barbie case and the plastic compartment.

I picked up the swan and studied it. The wings on my bird were folded against its body, and I wondered idly if I'd ever be able to carve one with outstretched wings, like the master woodcarver had. After selecting the right-sized V-tool, I curled up

Indian fashion on the couch and set to work.

An hour or so later, Punky came into the living room, wearing his "Surf Bum" T-shirt and clean red jogging pants. His eyes were still puffy from sleep and he needed a shave. "Mornin', pretty girl," he said.

I grinned. Punky was the only person in the world who would ever think of me as pretty. "Hi. Hungry for breakfast?"

"I'm starved," he said, sitting down and turning on the television.

"Is cereal okay?"

"Nope. Bacon, two eggs, and toast. Shirley said."

"Well, then, clean off your table while I get it ready."

"Wait a minute."

I fried bacon and eggs and made toast, and then carried our food into the living room. Punky was watching TV with the sound off and listening to his new radio. His crayon pieces were in the basket, but now the six clowns were lined up like sentries at the far edge of the table.

Punky ate slowly, taking a bite now and then as he switched channels from cartoons to commercials and back again. When at last he finished eating, I decided it was time to clean up the mess. "Sorry, Punky," I said as I dragged the vacuum cleaner from the closet, "this room is a pigpen."

"Okay, D.J.," he replied, placing the clowns in his lunch box and heading for the back door with the lunch box and the radio.

After unwinding the cord on the sweeper, I glanced outside. He was lining up a row of lawn chairs in front of his swing set for a make-believe audience.

I shook the sheet full of wood shavings out the front door and collected the horns from behind the TV. There were ten of them, all dry and hard and covered with fuzzies, and I laughed. If Queen Esther Holloway could see them, she'd throw a royal fit.

Later I went out to check on Punky. He was singing, holding his pretend microphone to his mouth and his radio to one ear. The sunshine made his whiskers glisten.

I sat in the other swing, wondering how it would feel to be like Punky, without a worry in the world.

Now that he had a live audience, he began swinging higher and singing louder, making up a song about Jellybean and Santa Claus and Uncle Bert all rolled into one.

I dug my bare feet into the soft dirt under the swing and watched it sift up between my long, skinny toes.

"Did you get a new radio?" someone asked, and I spun around to see the bratty Gregory kid spying on us.

"Hey, boy, what are you doing here?" I demanded, jumping off the swing as he jumped off his bike.

"I just wanted to see where the music was coming

from. Is that against the law?" he replied, staring at Punky.

"My radio, my present," Punky said proudly.

"It's against the law to trespass on private property," I snapped.

The brat continued to stare at Punky.

"I *said* it's against the law—"

"I heard what you said. I just . . ."

"Just what?"

The boy sputtered, "I just wondered—I mean—I—I didn't know he had whiskers."

I snorted my disgust. "Of course he's got whiskers! He's thirty-five years old!"

"But he swings and plays."

"So he's not like other people. That doesn't give you the right to come snooping around all the time. This isn't a sideshow."

"I don't snoop."

"Oh, yes you do. You even bring your friends."

"I'm sorry about that," said the boy, scuffing the toes of his tennis shoes. "When they hear Punky singing, they want to see what he looks like."

Punky didn't appreciate being left out of the conversation. He opened his lunch box and showed off his clowns.

"Hey, those are neat," said the boy. "We could play circus."

"Circus. Yeah!" said Punky, clapping his hands.

"I don't think so." This was getting too complicated, and I didn't know what to do. I couldn't remember anybody besides me ever wanting to play with Punky. Most little kids were afraid of him or just wanted somebody to laugh at.

"Couldn't I play for a few minutes?" asked the boy.

I studied his face and decided maybe he did just want to play. He was only a second-grader, and if he started acting like a brat, I was bigger than he was. "All right, boy," I said, "but I'll be watching you from the house."

I turned to go inside, and he called after me, "Marcus."

"What?"

"My name isn't Boy. It's Marcus."

I moved my carving things to the kitchen so I could keep an eye on the backyard. With the slightest twinge of jealousy, I listened to Marcus and Punky giggling and playing together in the dirt under the swing set.

I scolded myself as I worked on the swan. Why shouldn't Punky have a friend? After all, *he* wasn't invisible.

There were times I wished he were invisible, like when we went to church and he sang the hymns too loud with his pretend microphone. Or when he saw the flag at the post office and stopped dead in the middle of the street to salute.

I thought about the last time our family went to see a Walt Disney movie. Punky had gnawed at his fingers until they were all slobbery, and he twisted his hair into wet spikes. Every few minutes, he'd clap his hands and say, "Look, D.J.!"

My face turned hot at the memory of everybody in the theater staring at us and snickering.

I was gouging too hard at the swan, and suddenly I broke off the neck. I felt like crying, not because of the broken hunk of wood, but because I was ashamed of my shame. Punky couldn't help being the way he was.

I rounded off the neck, then marched into Punky's bedroom and plunked the deformed duck down beside the other animals on the shelf.

Frowning with frustration, I glanced around the room that represented Punky's little-boy world. There were clowns on the curtains and bedspread and wallpaper, and clown posters on every wall. By the dresser was a big punching-bag clown, leering at me. I slugged him hard, wanting him to fall down and stay down, but he bounced back up on his balloon bottom and continued to leer.

When the cooing sound of Punky's laughter drifted through the open window, my frustration drifted away, too. I went back to the shelf, swept all the animals into the bottom of my T-shirt, and carried them outside.

Marcus and Punky were making the clowns do tricks. Marcus had broken out with more freckles, and Punky's bald spot had turned pink from sunburn.

As my shadow crossed over Punky, he looked up at me, all smiles, his whiskery moon face streaked with grime.

Marcus narrowed his eyes at me and wiped a hand

across his forehead, making little dirt balls in the sweat. "We're doing okay," he said quickly, as if he expected me to give him a hard time.

"I know," I replied as I knelt down to dump my burden. "I just thought of something. You can't have a really great circus without animals."

SIX

The Whistle

I heard Marcus's mother calling him home to eat, so I started fixing lunch for Punky and me.

When Marcus left a few minutes later, Punky came in the back door, saying, "I'm starved."

"I know," I said, dropping ice cubes into a clown glass and filling it with tea.

Punky grabbed the tea and chugged it down while I said, "Wash your hands and face. The hamburgers'll be done in a jiffy."

"Yeah, D.J."

Soon I heard a suspicious sloshing in the bathroom, and in a flash I knew Mom had forgotten to hide the shampoo. Punky wouldn't touch a full bottle of shampoo, but as soon as it reached the halfway mark—whoosh! down the toilet! I shot into the bathroom, but he was already replacing the cap on the empty bottle.

"Gone," he said as he held the bottle up to the

light and looked at the rainbow of bubbles.

I groaned. How was I going to wash my hair?

After lunch, I told Punky we had to get more shampoo, and sent him in to shave.

"Oh, boy," he said, heading for the bathroom.

I shook my head sadly. I hated going to the store with Punky, because I never knew when he'd take something. He didn't mean to steal, but his idea of a fair trade was to swap one of his treasures for an item he liked on a store shelf.

After I'd cleaned off the table, I took Punky's medicine down from the cupboard and stuffed it in my pocket. It was nitroglycerin, the same ingredient used in dynamite. Punky and dynamite. What a combination.

He came out of the bathroom, plastering his hair down with a wet washcloth.

"Ready?" I asked.

"Wait a minute," he replied, puttering off to his bedroom, his lunch box under his arm.

I followed, knowing it wouldn't have made any difference if the house were on fire. He wouldn't set foot outside until he had packed his belongings. I didn't offer to help, though, because of the unwritten rule—hands off the cowboy hat and the lunch box.

Punky opened the box and removed all the clowns except Jellybean. In their place went the clown glass, a handful of broken crayons, and a small American flag. I'd have to watch him like a hawk, to be sure he didn't make a swap. When he had donned his cowboy hat and admired himself in the mirror, he said, "Ready."

I didn't dare hurry Punky, because of his heart and the heat, so we poked along to the highway. At the intersection, workmen were eating lunch in the shell of an unfinished building.

"Hi, boys," Punky called.

The men laughed, and I felt their eyes boring into us as we passed.

Half a block from the supermarket, I said, "Remember now, all we want is shampoo. No dog biscuits, no toilet bowl cleaner, no toothpaste or aftershave."

"Yeah, D.J."

The store's big door opened automatically when we stepped on the mat. Punky never could figure out how the door knew we were coming, and it always made him giggle.

I took his arm, intending to steer him toward the beauty aisle, but he stopped at a lighted glass cubicle beside the gumball machines. "Look, D.J. Chinny," he said.

Inside the cubicle was a big plastic chicken, sitting on a mound of plastic eggs. For a quarter, the sign said, the chicken would lay an egg and you would get a prize.

I gave him a quarter, which he fed into the coin slot. The light in the cubicle started flashing, and the chicken flapped its wings and let out a series of terrible squawks. Every egg in the case shifted as one purple egg clattered down a chute.

My cheeks burned with embarrassment as customers and cashiers turned to see the commotion.

Punky laughed and clapped his hands. He pried open the egg, which held a green plastic whistle on a string. Before I could stop him, he stuck the whistle in his mouth and blew—a loud, shrill sound that scared him and made my stomach lurch.

I grabbed Punky's arm and steered him down the nearest aisle. My heart was pumping fast. If I have a heart attack, I thought grimly, at least there's nitroglycerin in my pocket.

"You have it," Punky said, thrusting the whistle at me.

I took it, grateful beyond words that he didn't want to blow it again. After snatching up a bottle of shampoo, I hustled Punky to the checkout lane. Thank goodness, he was satisfied with his purple egg. The last thing I needed was for someone to accuse us of shoplifting.

Mom and Dad came home with several antiques for the shop but without the roll-top desk.

"It brought twelve hundred dollars!" said Mom, sinking into a chair in the kitchen. She and Dad were both so sunburned they looked like they'd been fried in hot oil.

Punky came up behind Mom and kissed the top of her head. He placed his hands on her shoulders and said, "Hi, pretty girl."

Grimacing from the pain, she eased his hands away. "How's Punky?"

"I'm starved."

"Punky Holloway, you're always starved," said Mom, laughing.

"How about if we eat at McDonald's?" Dad suggested.

"Yeah," said Punky. "Big Mac."

I didn't say anything. There'd be too many people out on Saturday night to suit me.

There were three flagpoles outside the restaurant, flying the American flag, the Missouri flag, and the McDonald's banner. As usual, Punky paused to salute.

The place was crowded, but I didn't see anybody I recognized. There were mostly families with small children, all sunburned as if they'd spent the day at the Lake of the Ozarks.

Mom and I told Dad what we wanted, and went to find a booth. Punky stayed with Dad, and I could see him showing off his coupons to customers in the line.

One lady smiled at him, but the small boy she was holding piped, "Mama, what's the matter with that little man?" The lady turned away quickly and told her son to hush. Another customer, a wrinkled old woman with bleached hair, short shorts, and six pounds of makeup, moved to a different line. To me, she looked stranger than Punky.

Punky came to the table and said, "Look, D.J., clown," as he showed me a plastic soft-drink cup with Ronald McDonald's picture on the side. When he sat down, he stashed a couple of packets of ketchup in his lunch box.

Seeing the purple egg, Mom asked, "Did you go somewhere today?"

"The supermarket. We were out of shampoo."

Mom raised her eyebrows at Punky.

"Gone," he said, dipping a french fry in ketchup, then popping it into his mouth.

Punky took forever to eat, and I was nervous. I wanted to get out of there before a school crowd arrived.

School. I still had to do math homework, and Avanelle had the book. She'd said she lived behind McDonald's, and this seemed as good a time as any to find out where.

"I'm supposed to get a book from Avanelle Shackleford," I said, sliding out of the booth. "She lives right over there. I'll be back in a minute."

I ran through the parking lot and cut across somebody's backyard, hoping it was Avanelle's. I went around to the front of the house and was sure of it. The yard was swarming with redheaded, freckle-faced kids. They had to be part of a matched set.

"Who are you?" asked a little girl who looked to be about four.

"My name's Delrita," I said, noticing the peeling paint on the house and the broken rails on the porch. "I'm looking for Avanelle. Is she home?"

The girl stuck her thumb in her mouth and sized me up with her emerald eyes before answering, "Uh-huh."

"Would you get her, please?"

By then the whole clan had gathered around me.

"Would one of you please get Avanelle?"

Nobody moved, and I began to feel like Custer, surrounded by Indians at his last stand. Only these Indians had carrot-colored hair with masses of tight curls—the kind my dad called "moptops."

"Are you the lady from the welfare office?" demanded a tough little guy of about six.

"No, I'm a friend of Avanelle's. From school."

"She don't have any friends here," said Tough Guy.

"She didn't have any friends in St. Louis, either," volunteered another boy, slightly bigger.

No wonder Avanelle wanted to come to my house to study. "Look," I said, "Avanelle's in my class at school, and she's got my math book."

Still the kids didn't budge. They just stood staring at me with a haunted look in their eyes.

At last someone rescued me by sticking her head out the screen door and calling, "Randolph, who you talking to?"

I turned and looked at the woman, who was obviously the mother of this clan, because she, too, had freckles and a head full of tight red curls. Her bulging stomach pushed against the screen, and I realized she was expecting another little moptop to feed.

"I'm Delrita Jensen," I said. "I'm looking for Avanelle. She's got my math book."

"Well, come on in and I'll get her."

I went inside, followed by the whole gang from

the yard. The small living room seemed crowded, not because it was filled with furniture, but because of all the people in it. There wasn't much furniture at all—just a dingy old chair, a couch hidden under a raggedy quilt, and a coffee table marred with burns and scratches. The room was clean, but the pole lamp in the corner didn't have a shade, and its bare bulb cast a harsh glare.

I remembered hearing a joke once about people on welfare having color TVs and Cadillacs, but that wasn't the case at this house.

"Delrita?" said Avanelle, coming into the room ahead of her mother. Her face was flushed, as if she were embarrassed to have me there.

"I—I just came to get the math book. If you're finished." I understood her embarrassment. How many times had I been embarrassed about Punky?

"Yes," said Avanelle, handing me the book but not meeting my gaze. "I didn't know when you'd show up, so I did my homework last night. Converting decimals to fractions. It's hard."

It occurred to me that maybe Avanelle had tried all day to keep the living room clean, so it wouldn't look bad when I came. Even with all these kids, there wasn't a toy or a dirty dish in sight, but there was a fresh bouquet of brown-eyed susans in a quart jar on the coffee table.

"I'm sorry," I said. "From now on I'll do my math in study hall so we won't have to worry about the book."

"What'd you say your name was?" asked Avanelle's mother, smiling at me.

"Delrita. Delrita Jensen."

"Honey, you didn't mention anybody by that name," said Mrs. Shackleford.

"There wasn't anything to say," replied Avanelle, and I felt a pang of guilt. There might have been something to say if I hadn't been so unfriendly.

"I'd better go," I said. "My folks are waiting for me."

"Okay," mumbled Avanelle. "See you Monday at school."

The little girl who sucked her thumb followed me onto the porch. "You have a pretty name," she said.

"I do?" As far as I knew, nobody but my parents had ever liked the name Delrita. "Thank you. What's your name?"

"Birdie."

"Birdie? You mean like a bird that flies?"

"No. Birdie. Gil-birdie."

"Oh, Gilberta. That's a pretty name, too."

"Will you come back and see us?"

"I don't think so."

"'Cause my daddy stoled?"

"What?"

"'Cause my daddy stoled and the police comed and took him to jail?"

"No," I said, confused. "I—I—I just don't visit other people."

"Why?"

"I just don't," I said uncomfortably, jamming my

free hand into my pocket. My fingers closed around something small and hard, and I pulled it out. It was Punky's whistle.

Birdie's eyes lit up when she saw it, but she didn't say a word. She was probably used to seeing things she couldn't have.

"Here, Birdie," I said, placing the string around her neck. "This is just your size."

She lifted the whistle to admire it, and I turned to go.

I was at the corner of the house when I heard a loud, shrill blast. I looked back and waved, and Birdie called, "Bye, Velveeta."

"Who is Avanelle?" Mom asked when I got back to McDonald's. "Is she in your class? How long has she lived in Tangle Nook?"

All evening, she kept hinting that I should invite Avanelle over to the house. I knew she just wanted me to have a friend, but she nearly worried me to death.

I went to sleep thinking about Mr. Shackleford's being in jail, and I dreamed that Avanelle stole my purse out of my locker. We had a hair-pulling fight, and Birdie jumped out of the locker and started blowing on a whistle. Students formed a circle around us and taunted Avanelle, "Thief and liar, hair's on fire!" When the principal came to break up the fight, all he saw was Avanelle writhing around by herself, because I was invisible.

SEVEN

The Moptops

On Sunday morning, I pulled back the curtain and saw clouds gathering as if they meant business. I hoped it wouldn't rain. Rain and organ music were the only two things I could think of that made Punky cry—probably because he associated them with monster shows on TV.

After showering and washing my hair, I hid the shampoo out of habit, even though the bottle was brand-new.

I dressed in a light green blouse and a denim skirt with a ruffle on the bottom that did a fair job of hiding my skinny legs. Pulling the sides of my hair up into a barrette, I let the rest of it hang straight and loose down my back.

In the living room, Punky was rolling crayons on his sawed-off table, watching TV, and trying to tune the static out of his radio. "Call the news," he said. "Don't want no rain."

I picked up the telephone and pretended to dial. "Hello, KRCG-TV Thirteen? This is Delrita Jensen in Tangle Nook. I'm calling for Mr. Punky Holloway, who is tired of you guys fooling around with the weather. He wants sunshine every day until Christmas, and then you can throw in a little snow. What's that? Okay, I'll give him the message."

"Oh boy," said Punky as I hung up the receiver. "Snow, Christmas, Santy Claus."

"The weatherman said to tell you they have to clean out the clouds once in a while, but they'll try not to do it on our house."

"Thank you, D.J.," replied Punky, selecting more crayons from his basket.

Later, in the car on the way to church, I stared out the window of the backseat and let my thoughts wander. Why hadn't Avanelle had friends in St. Louis? How long had her father been in jail?

As we passed the school, Mom said, "It can't be much fun for Avanelle, being the new kid in eighth grade. You've said yourself that school has so many cliques." She looked at me hopefully, her eyes asking me to please make friends with Avanelle.

Mom was thirty-seven years old and didn't have one close friend, but what bothered her was that I didn't, either. She hadn't ever had many friends, and she'd survived it. I would, too.

Mom was the oldest of four children, and life on the farm had been hectic after Grandpa died and Grandma went to work at a factory.

"I never had a chance to be a kid," she always said. "I had to grow up too fast."

Right after graduating from high school, Mom married Dad, who was five years older than she was. Shortly afterward, Grandma died and my folks moved into the farmhouse to take care of Punky, then sixteen, and the two younger children. Bert and Donna finished school and went their own ways, but Mom was left in charge of Punky.

If she ever resented having all the responsibility, she never let on, but she sure made it rough on me. "I want it to be different for you, Delrita," she'd said a dozen times. "I want you to play tennis in the park, swim in the pool, join the Scouts, and hang out with your friends."

I must have been a disappointment to my mother. I'd never been very good at making friends or shown much interest in activities away from the farm. I'd gone to school because I had to, and every day I'd hurried home to play with Punky. I'd thought that maybe in Tangle Nook things would be different, but now I was a total hermit.

It felt terrible not being able to tell Mom the truth—that I couldn't make friends with Avanelle because I was ashamed of Punky, thanks to Georgina's acting as if he were a creature from *Star Trek*.

Punky reached across the seat to straighten the ruffle on my skirt. "I love you, D.J.," he said, as he often did when I was blue. "You love me?"

"Sure do, handsome," I said, my mixed-up emotions eating me alive. How could I love Punky and be ashamed of him at the same time?

Punky grinned and adjusted his cowboy hat. He was wearing his best red jogging suit and new white sneakers that Mom had bought in the children's department at Wal-Mart, and he looked like one of Santa's roly-poly elves. I couldn't imagine what it was about him that would scare anybody.

"Looks like there's a pretty good crowd today," Mom said as Dad drove into the parking area of Countryside Church.

"Yeah," Dad replied, shutting off the motor. "Maybe twenty-five, thirty people, counting us and the preacher. I hope there's room for us to sit inside."

"Oh, Sam," said Mom, giving his arm a playful push.

The church had only an old upright piano, so there was no organ music to make Punky cry. The congregation was mostly old folks, and the preacher's three preschoolers and I were the only children. Sometimes I helped Mom teach the little ones, but usually I stayed in the sanctuary with the adults.

Brother Hicks was standing at the top of the steps, shaking hands with people as they came in.

Punky wasn't satisfied with just a handshake. He slapped the preacher on the back and said, "Hi, buddy," before going inside to greet everybody in sight.

I smiled when he hugged Miss Myrtle Chambers

and told her she was a pretty girl. Miss Myrtle was a tiny, stooped woman of about eighty, but I knew what Punky meant by pretty. Everything about her reminded me of a delicate antique doll—onionskin flesh, faded blue eyes, wispy white hair, and a pastel dress that smelled faintly of lavender.

"Why, Punky, you make an old woman like me wish I was young again," said Miss Myrtle with a giggle.

"Hey, Punk-Man, that's my girl," boomed a voice behind me, and I turned and saw Uncle Bert. He and Aunt Queenie were members here, too, because Aunt Queenie believed that families should worship together.

"She's my girl, you old goat," said Punky, placing his hands on his hips.

"My girl," Uncle Bert said over his shoulder as Aunt Queenie pulled him toward a pew.

Catching up with Aunt Queenie, Punky said, "Hi, pretty girl," and thumped her on the back.

I didn't notice my aunt's reaction because just then I spied a whole row of carrot-colored moptops in a center pew. It couldn't be, but it was—the Shackleford family! Avanelle and her mother were trying to get the little ones to turn around and stop staring at us.

Sitting closest to the aisle was a boy I hadn't seen before, but he had to be Avanelle's older brother. His orangey-red hair was a tangle of curls, and the muscular arm resting along the back of the pew was spattered with freckles.

"Wonald McDonald," cried Punky, striding up to the boy and tousling his woolly hair.

As the boy glanced up in surprise, Punky ruffled his curls and said, "Hi, buddy. Clown hair. Like Wonald McDonald."

I grabbed Punky's arm and pulled him away, and mumbled, "I'm sorry." My face was on fire.

The boy was grinning at me, and there was a twinkle in his eyes. "I've been called a ragtop and a frizzhead, but I've never been mistaken for a clown," he said.

"Hi, Velveeta," piped a voice, and I looked down the pew and saw six pairs of eyes fixed on me. Avanelle was gazing curiously, her mother was smiling, but Birdie was jiggling in her seat and waving.

"Velveeta?" said the boy. "And I thought I had a strange name—Trezane. All my friends call me Tree."

I couldn't even tell him my name wasn't Velveeta. My mouth felt crammed with melted cheese, and my brain wouldn't work.

Punky was straining to get away from me. At last Mom took him to a seat a couple of rows down, and Dad shook hands with as many Shacklefords as he could reach.

I wanted to run out of the church and never come back, but I knew that wouldn't work. Punky would just come looking for me, and I'd have some explaining to do to my parents. I crept up to sit beside Punky, who clapped his hands happily at being in church.

The opening exercises seemed to last forever, with Punky singing the hymns off-key into his pretend microphone. Every time someone said "Amen," Punky responded with "Bang!" The regular members had gotten used to it, but I figured the Shacklefords were laughing at Punky behind our backs.

When the little kids were dismissed to go to their class, Brother Hicks asked everyone else to move forward. Tree came up and sat beside me, followed by his mother and Avanelle.

Punky snapped open his lunch box to look at his treasures. The crayon pieces and the clowns rolled around in the box, and Punky punched me and pointed, to show me that his flag was exactly like the one at the front of the church.

I nodded, hoping against hope that the Shacklefords were paying attention to the preacher and not to Punky.

When the service was over, I couldn't escape because of the people on both sides of me.

Avanelle just smiled shyly, but her mother and Tree wanted to talk.

"I feel at home in your church, Delrita," said Mrs. Shackleford as she folded her arms across her swollen stomach. "I think we'll be back next Sunday."

"Delrita Velveeta." Tree chuckled and glanced down at me. I studied his emerald eyes, but there was nothing to suggest that he would poke fun at Punky. "You're the one who gave Birdie the whistle."

"Delrita's in Avanelle's class," explained his

mother. "I'm surprised you didn't see her at school."

"The ninth-grade lockers are at the opposite end of the hall," replied Tree. "Besides, the guys said Coach gets mad if we don't show up for football practice within two minutes after the last bell."

Judging by the size of him, I should have guessed he was a football player. Now that I had gotten over my embarrassment enough to really look at him, I could see he was wearing a new blue and white jersey that said "Tangle Nook Wildcats." I wondered if he had chosen to wear it because he was proud to be on the team or because it was the best shirt he had. His jeans were worn at the knees, like the ones Avanelle wore to school.

"Are you coming to the game Friday night?" asked Tree.

"Oh, uh, I don't usually go to the games. I don't know that much about sports." Would he think I was an oddball if he knew I'd never even been to a game?

As we moved out of the pew, the little Shacklefords came running up to their mother to show her the Bible pictures they'd colored. One of the kids pulled on her dress, stretching it tight across her middle.

Punky followed me into the aisle and started teasing Birdie, running a hand through her curls and calling her "moptop."

I expected her to scream and run, but she didn't. Instead, she stuck her thumb in her mouth and showed her picture to Punky, all the time looking at him with big, round eyes.

Just when I was beginning to like this family, Punky did something to make me remember I was supposed to be invisible. He laughed, patted Mrs. Shackleford on the tummy, and said, "You're fat."

The words felt like a slap across my face. I raced down the aisle, out of the church, and lunged for the car. It was suffocating because the sun had come out, and I cranked down the window furiously. How stupid I had been to let my guard down, even for a minute, since I already knew my life could never be normal.

Tree came to the door of the building and stood peering toward the parking lot.

I slid to the floor and prayed that he wouldn't find me. Scrunching down with the floorboards gouging into my knees, I realized that I was being silly—hiding out like a criminal. Still, though, I stayed low. When I heard people talking and cars starting, I knew I had to get up. I eased upward and peeked out the window.

A beat-up station wagon was pulling out of the lot, and a moptop girl leaned out the window and blew a farewell toot on a whistle.

Miss Myrtle, who was being helped to a car by Elsie Golden, waved to Birdie. "Nice family," she said. "It's too bad the father didn't come to church with them. The mother looks worn-out."

"I should think so," clucked Elsie. "I didn't think anybody but Catholics had that many kids anymore.

And you could tell by looking at them that they're poor. Their clothes were—"

"Clean, starched, and ironed," interrupted Miss Myrtle, "not like some of the kids you see nowadays, who look like they've been run through the wringer."

Good for you, Miss Myrtle, I thought, and then wondered why it made any difference to me.

EIGHT

Spirit Week

I forgave Punky for embarrassing me, but I couldn't forgive myself for running away from Tree. What would I say if I saw him again? "My dinner was burning"? "My beeper beeped and I had to make a call"?

As I walked to school on Monday, I thought how Tree and Avanelle were a whole lot nicer than any other kids I'd run into in Tangle Nook. Maybe they had to be, if they wanted to fit in with the crowd. I wondered what it would be like to be poor, to wear faded clothes that hadn't been bought that way, and to have your father in jail.

When I got to school and saw all the posters and blue and white streamers in the hall, I remembered it was Spirit Week.

Students were supposed to dress up in a different kind of costume each day to show support for the football team. Today was Hawaiian Day, and nearly everyone was wearing wild flowered shirts, sunglasses, and floppy straw hats.

In English, first hour, when all the kids in Hawaiian clothes stood up to be counted, no one noticed that I wasn't in costume. How could they? I asked myself. I'm invisible. Anyway, they were all too interested in Cindi Martin, who was wearing a silk flower in her hair and dancing the hula in a grass skirt.

Next I had study hall, which seemed like a terrible waste. Who needed a study hall second hour? Then I remembered promising Avanelle I'd do math in study hall from now on. Today's assignment was finished, so I'd start tomorrow.

I sat daydreaming about Silver Dollar City. It was one of the few places where I didn't worry about people making fun of Punky. Maybe it was because they were so busy gawking at the sights they were too busy to gawk at anything else.

I doodled in my notebook, listing things I most wanted to see and do on Saturday, like watch the master woodcarver and ride the roller coaster called Fire-in-the-Hole.

When the bell rang, I went to my locker and exchanged the notebook for a sketch pad. Before I knew it, I was moseying toward the water fountain in the ninth-grade hallway, peeking in every classroom as I passed. What would I do if I spotted Tree or he spotted me? Would he even recognize me, since I'd washed and blow-dried my hair and styled it with a curling iron? When I reached the fountain,

I still hadn't found Tree, so I took a quick drink and hurried back the other way.

I must have looked like an owl, I thought, the way I was twisting my head from side to side. I smiled at the mental image. An owl looking for a Tree.

I expected to see Avanelle in art class, but I didn't expect to see her in Hawaiian clothes. She was wearing what looked like a flowered maternity dress, all wadded up around her waist with a belt.

"Hi, Delrita," she said eagerly. I could tell by her expression that she wished she hadn't dressed up like that for school.

"Hi," I said, my voice squeaky because she was the first person who had spoken to me since I'd walked into the building.

The way the other kids ignored her that hour gave me an odd sense of relief. At least I wouldn't have to worry about her blabbing to anybody about Punky.

At lunchtime, I sat alone in my usual spot and toyed with my Poor Man's Casserole. How the cooks could take perfectly good beef and vegetables and stir them up into a tasteless mess was beyond me. I wondered if they had special training in how to turn school food into glue.

"Does it taste as bad as it looks?" asked Avanelle, setting her tray down and pulling out a chair across from me.

"I don't know. I've been afraid to try it."

"I think I'll stick with the Jell-O and the bread and butter," Avanelle said as she unwrapped a straw and stuck it in her milk.

I felt suddenly bashful, as if she'd know somehow that I'd been in the ninth-grade hallway looking for her brother. Concentrating on the casserole, I chased it around on my tray.

Avanelle broke the silence by saying, "How'd you get the name Delrita?"

Nobody had ever asked me that before, so I hadn't dreamed up a fancy explanation. I decided to tell the truth and hope she wouldn't laugh like a hyena right here in the cafeteria. "It's a combination of my grandparents' names—Delbert and Margarita."

Avanelle didn't laugh. She looked thoughtful and said, "That's neat. When I came to this school, it seemed like all the girls have cutesy names spelled with an *i*—Cindi, Debbi, Tami, Bobbi—so when Miss Morley said I was supposed to share a math book with Delrita Jensen, I wanted to jump up and holler 'Hoo-ray!'"

"My middle name's Jolena, after my other set of grandparents. What's yours?" I asked, realizing too late that I was encouraging this conversation.

"Thurston."

"Thurston?"

"My mom's maiden name." Avanelle started giggling and said, "There's not a whole lot we can do with names like ours."

"You could go by Nelli. Nelli with an *i*."

"No, I've been that route. In St. Louis, kids called me Nelly-belly. I even tried Nell, and they called me Nell's Bells."

I grinned as she rattled on. "My mom goes for the

old-fashioned names. Trezane, Avanelle, Randolph, Edward, Gilberta, and Gordon. Even the new baby will be named Chandler or Elmira." Wrinkling her nose, she added, "Aren't those awful?"

"There's a city in New York called Elmira."

"Don't tell my mom that," said Avanelle.

In spite of myself, I laughed. "Elmira New York Shackleford. That would be a mouthful, all right."

Avanelle laughed, too, but then she looked serious. "Tree's named after our dad, but I think my mom gave all of us important-sounding names so we'd live up to them. You know—make something of ourselves."

I thought about the Shacklefords living in that shabby house while they waited for their dad to get out of jail, and instantly I felt sorry for the whole family.

Avanelle poked at her Jell-O with a spoon and said, "You sure made a hit with my sister. She keeps talking about Velveeta giving her a whistle."

"It wasn't any big deal."

"It was to her. It was something brand-new and shiny for a change." She paused a moment before going on. "Since you've seen where we live, you might as well know the rest of the Shackleford saga."

I glanced sharply at her. Was she going to tell me that her dad was in jail?

"We're used to getting old clothes from the welfare office and handouts from the government, but it's not very often that somebody gives us something brand-new just to be nice. Even at Christmastime, we get used toys that have been fixed up and painted."

I didn't want to hear any more of this depressing story, but I didn't know how to stop her. This was private information—the kind you'd tell only to your best friend—and Avanelle and I barely knew each other. Besides that, if she reported all this bad stuff about her own family, what would she report to other people about mine?

Avanelle's face was so white that her freckles seemed to stand up by themselves, and her fingers were ripping a paper napkin to shreds. Finally she gave me a weak smile and said, "I guess you're wondering why I'm telling you all this. In St. Louis, I was really backward around other people because of—uh, certain things. When we moved here, I tried hard to be different—more outgoing. Friday afternoon, when you didn't want to talk, I thought it was because of *me*. Now I know it was because of that little man who was with you at church. You were trying to hide him, weren't you?"

"No. Yes. Oh, I don't know," I mumbled, staring at the table. "Punky's my uncle. He lives with us. He—he's different."

"He was funny. On the way home, we laughed about him telling Mom she's fat. He's right, you know. She has to tape a poker chip over her belly button to keep it from poking through her clothes."

So they had laughed at Punky after all. I felt strangely disappointed.

Avanelle gave a deep sigh. "All families have secrets. I guess some of us just have worse secrets than others."

Avanelle ate lunch with me every day that week. Since we had PE fourth hour and lunch right after that, it worked out that we were walking together to the cafeteria anyway.

She didn't mention Punky again, so I just let her chatter on and nodded in the appropriate places. She talked mostly about the outfits the kids were wearing to school.

Tuesday was Pajama Day, followed by Backward Day, Movie Star Day, and Opposite-Sex Day. Some of the costumes were downright ridiculous, and it was a relief to go home, where everything was normal, where we hid the shampoo and had horn bones behind the TV.

By Friday, it was obvious that no one was learning anything in any classes, and the whole school was wound up tight over the big game. At the afternoon pep rally, I was already penned in on the bleachers when Avanelle came into the gym. Wearing Tree's football jersey, which was about fourteen sizes too big for her, she looked small and forlorn as she tried to find a seat.

The coach introduced the football players, and they lumbered onto the gym floor in makeup and jewelry and pillow-stuffed gowns. For once, I was one of the crowd, laughing out loud with my classmates, especially at Tree in a feathery tent dress, tottering along on high heels.

★   ★   ★

When the last bell rang and everyone swarmed out of the building, storm clouds boiled in the sky and thunder rumbled from west to east like low-flying jets. The air, which had hung hot and heavy in the classrooms all afternoon, suddenly turned cold, as if someone had opened a giant refrigerator.

Since I didn't have a jacket, I hoped I could beat the rain. I was trying to decide whether to detour or wait for the buses to move when someone caught my arm and asked, "Are you coming to the game?"

I looked around and saw Tree. "You mean you'll play, even if it rains?"

"Sure," he said. "Coach says it'll make men out of us."

That struck me as hilarious, coming from a boy whose eyelids were glistening with silver makeup and whose cheeks were smeared with rouge. I started laughing and couldn't stop.

Tree laughed, too—a deep, rumbly sound that reminded me of rocks being tossed in a barrel. "Kids have been telling me all day that I look funny, but nobody got hysterical over it," he said.

I held my sides as the laughter slowly bubbled down into giggles. At last I managed to gasp, "You—you—you really could pass for Ronald Mc-Donald!"

Tree gave a sheepish grin. "I guess I should be offended, but I'm not. . . . How about it? Are you coming to the game?"

The laughter left me as quickly as it came. For

some strange reason, I *did* want to watch him play football. I wanted to scream and yell for Trezane Shackleford and the Tangle Nook Wildcats. But I couldn't—wouldn't—go.

Tree was watching me, waiting for an answer. I didn't know how to tell him no. He wouldn't understand what it was like to go someplace alone, to sit in a crowd with no one to talk to. I had had enough of that to last a lifetime, and I'd never forget riding a jam-packed bus on a field trip in May and having a whole seat to myself.

At last I thought of an excuse. "I can't be out that late," I said. "We're leaving early in the morning for Silver Dollar City."

"Oh," he said. "That's great. I've always wanted to go there."

"You girls are going to get wet," teased Avanelle, coming up behind us.

"Give me a break," moaned her brother.

I could have kicked myself. Why hadn't I thought to ask Avanelle to go with me to the game?

Fat raindrops plopped onto my cheek and rolled down my notebook. I glanced up as the drops came faster and shards of lightning split the sky, close enough to make me run for cover any other time.

"Come on," yelled Tree, "before we get soaked." He hobbled toward the school, as fast as he could go in his high heels. Avanelle and I started after him, but then I heard a car horn and looked back.

My mom had pulled her station wagon into the

spot the buses had just left, and she was hollering for us to jump in.

I hesitated for a second because Punky was with her in the front seat and he was crying. What would Tree and Avanelle think of him being scared of the rain?

"Hurry, Delrita," Mom called. "You other kids, too. I'll take you home."

Avanelle and Tree didn't wait to be asked again. They ran for the car and clambered into the backseat. There was nothing for me to do but crawl in beside Avanelle.

Punky forgot his fears for a moment when he saw Tree dressed like a girl. He turned around and said, "You're a clown."

"I know," agreed Tree. "Delrita just told me I look like Ronald McDonald."

"Delrita!" Mom said, catching my eye in the rearview mirror as she shifted the car into gear. I knew what she was thinking: No *wonder* you don't have any friends.

"It's all right," said Tree. "I asked for it, coming to school in this getup. Coach insisted the whole team dress up for Spirit Week."

Mom was still eyeing me in the mirror. Here it was Friday, and I hadn't even *mentioned* Spirit Week.

She stopped at a red light and said, "I was glad to see your family at church on Sunday."

"We liked it," said Tree. "It's a lot smaller than the one we went to in St. Louis."

The rain started pouring down as the light

changed, and Mom turned the windshield wipers on full blast.

With big tears rolling down his cheeks, Punky looked back at me and said, "Call the news, D.J. Don't want no rain."

I didn't say anything, so when the sky flickered with lightning, Punky shivered and said again, "Call the news."

I could feel the questioning stares of Tree and Avanelle, but right now I couldn't worry about them. Reaching across to pat Punky on the shoulder, I said, "I can't. I don't have a phone."

Tree and Avanelle exchanged glances, and Mom explained, "Punky thinks Delrita can call the weatherman and shut off the rain. In fact, he thinks she can do just about anything."

"Birdie would believe that," said Tree with a chuckle.

"Birdie was in my class last Sunday," said Mom. "She's quite a little talker."

"What did she talk about?" Avanelle asked quickly.

"Everything. She told me she swallowed a bolt and had to go to the hospital. And she said she had a chicken named Henrietta, but it got stolen."

"Oh," said Avanelle, obviously relieved.

"I'm curious about the bolt," Mom went on. "Did she have to have surgery?"

"No," answered Tree, and his face lit up with a grin. "The doctor said to think of it as a trial or tribulation. 'This, too, shall pass.'"

Mom chuckled at the doctor's joke, and I caught myself smiling.

Soon Mom turned off at McDonald's, and Tree directed her to the right house. He got out of the car but kept his head ducked inside as he thanked us for the ride and told Punky, "Don't worry about the storm. Pretend it's angels shooting fireworks in the sky."

He and Avanelle ran across the yard, and when they reached the porch, they turned and signaled Punky with their thumbs up.

I studied Tree, thinking how he'd been a real gentleman with Punky.

He waved at me and disappeared into the house, letting the door slam in his sister's face.

". . . seem like nice kids," Mom was saying as we drove away. "I met their mother at church. The poor woman has her hands full, with all those children and another one on the way. I wonder about her husband—where he is, where he works."

"Avanelle never said," I replied. Mom wasn't the kind of person who would judge the kids by their parents, so I don't know why I didn't tell her about Mr. Shackleford's being in jail.

By the time we got home, the rain had stopped and a watery sun was peeking out from behind the clouds.

Punky climbed out of the car, tipped his cowboy hat to the sky, and said, "Thank you, D.J." Then, tucking his lunch box under his arm, he headed for the house.

NINE

Silver Dollar City

After supper, I sketched another swan on cardboard and took it to the garage, where I asked Dad to cut some shapes for me out of basswood.

He uncovered his band saw and scratched his head thoughtfully as he looked at the drawing. "Why not do something different with this one?"

"Like what?"

"Open his wings."

"I'm not ready for that," I replied. "I haven't carved one yet without breaking its neck."

"If you break the whole batch, I can always cut more." Tossing a pencil to me, he said, "Come on, give this little fellow a chance. Let him spread his wings and fly."

Doubtfully, I sketched and erased and sketched some more.

Dad grinned when he saw my final drawing. "That's good. Now he'll look like a full-grown trumpeter, and not an ugly duckling."

I spent the rest of the evening holding a block of wood, but I didn't do much carving. I kept thinking about a certain pair of eyes. Green eyes. My favorite color.

When I went to bed, sleep was a long time coming. My mind worked overtime, thinking about Tree and Avanelle, and I was surprised to find I wanted to share Silver Dollar City with them.

Before daylight the next morning, we were sailing down Highway 65 South for the three-hour drive to Branson, pulling the furniture trailer behind us.

Punky slept most of the way. Time meant nothing to him, and even though we'd explained about getting up early, he'd stayed up to salute all the flags on TV.

I dozed for a while, but when the sun came up, I sat looking at the scenery and wondering idly if the Wildcats had beaten the Tigers at the game.

Punky was taking up about three-fourths of the backseat, his legs stretched out beside me and his head resting on a pillow in his lap. You'd think it would break his back, but even in his bed at home, he folded himself in half like that to sleep.

"Five more miles to Branson," said Dad at last, rubbing his neck and stretching his shoulders.

"Delrita, you'd better wake Punky," Mom said.

I ruffled the hair around Punky's bald spot, where he was the most ticklish. He quivered a little and grunted.

"Time to wake up."

"Wait a minute."

"Come on, sleepyhead. We're almost there."

"Wait a minute."

This went on for about three miles before Punky roused enough to sit upright. Even then he kept his eyes closed against the glaring sun and bobbled lazily like a buoy in the water.

Mischievously, I reached for his Jellybean lunch box and said, "If you leave this in the car, you won't have to lug it around all day."

"Hey, you rascal, hands off," said Punky, instantly alert as he snatched the box from me. He checked its contents carefully—two clowns, a flag, his red birthday socks, a handful of broken crayons, and the Ronald McDonald cup. Then he folded his arms and pouted, his chin jutting out so far that his bottom lip covered his top lip and he resembled a little old man with no teeth.

"Punky's mad, and I'm sad, and I know what'll please him," I said, chanting the rhyme that I used when I knew I'd gone too far, "—a bottle of ink to make him stink, a bottle of wine to make him shine, and a barrel of monkeys to tease him."

"Don't want no monkeys," said Punky, but there was a hint of a smile in his eyes.

"You smell good this morning," I said. "What's that after-shave?"

"Sam say," replied Punky, jerking a thumb toward Dad.

Dad's eyes met mine in the rearview mirror. "It's Wicked Cowboy," he said. "Just right for sweeping dance-hall girls off their feet."

"Yeah, buddy," said Punky, shining the silver trim

on his cowboy hat with the sleeve of his jogging jacket. His grumpy mood was already past, and he was ready for action. I grinned at the thought. At best, Punky's action would be in slow motion.

When we got close to the auction arena, a guard stopped us from going into the parking lot. "It's full," he said. "You'll have to park here on the main road and walk in."

Dad thanked him and turned to Mom. "Do you want to get out here? No sense in all of us wearing out our shoe leather. We've got to save some for— Hey! Why don't we take these two hooligans on to Silver Dollar City? We could meet up with them this afternoon, after you and I have looked at antiques."

"Let's do it, Dad," I said eagerly, hanging over the back of his seat.

"I don't know," Mom said. "That's a lot of responsibility for Delrita."

"I can handle it."

"Shirley, it just makes sense. Punky would be bored to tears around all that furniture, and think of the Depression glass and expensive crystal."

Mom gave in at the mention of the glassware. Punky was clumsy, and one wrong step could cost several hundred dollars in damage. "Well, okay," she said, and Dad swung the car back onto the highway.

Silver Dollar City was nine miles from Branson on a winding, hilly stretch of Route 76. The view to our left was breathtaking—hills and valleys in countless fall colors, all muted by the morning mist rising off Table Rock Lake. In some places, the guardrails along the road's edge seemed like small protection from sheer drop-offs into empty space.

Dad kept glancing in the rearview mirror. "Bringing that trailer into these hills wasn't such a good idea. It's top-heavy without a load, and I can feel it bucking against us every time I touch the brakes."

"It's creepy," I said, "like riding Fire-in-the-Hole."

Mom shot me a worried look. "Don't take Punky on that ride. It's dangerous for anybody with a weak heart."

"I know. I'll go later with Dad."

She gave me the bottle of nitroglycerin and a whole list of dos and don'ts. "Don't let Punky out of your sight. . . . Don't let him get too tired. . . . If it gets hot, go inside where it's air-conditioned and watch a stage show. . . . Remember, there's a first-aid station across from the blacksmith shop."

Finally, Dad steered into the Silver Dollar City parking area and stopped. He gave me fifty dollars—the most I'd ever held at one time—and said with a wink, "Don't spend it all in one place."

Mom checked her watch and said, "We'll meet you at two o'clock at the general store."

Punky and I got out, and as Dad backed the trailer into a parking space so he could turn around, Mom hung out the window, blowing kisses and hollering, "Have fun!"

Our tickets cost thirty-six dollars, but they would entitle us to go on all the rides and see all the shows as often as we wanted. Thinking how fifty dollars wasn't much money after all, I jammed the remaining fourteen into my jeans pocket with the ten-dollar bill I'd brought from home.

Punky, gripping his lunch box with one hand and me with the other, tugged me toward the music and laughter and friendly atmosphere that was Silver Dollar City.

The place was bustling with people in old-fashioned costumes, from cowboys with six-guns and leather chaps to dance-hall girls with plumed hats, frilly dresses, and button-topped shoes.

At the gazebo, a band was playing bluegrass music, and a character who called himself Sheriff Howdy Highpockets was handing out badges to little kids. Punky marched right up to get a badge of his own and stood grinning as I pinned it to his T-shirt.

I was itching to go to the woodcarving shop, but I figured Punky would be easier to keep track of if I tired him out first. Besides, the City was already crowded, and the lines for the rides would get longer as the day wore on.

First we rode the steam-engine train, where Punky's hat was "stolen" by a band of robbers. "Hands off," he ordered when he finally got it back.

We rode the water toboggan and took a float trip through the flooded mine before the warm, spicy smell of simmering apple butter convinced us it was time to eat.

After a thirteen-dollar lunch at the Lumbercamp

Restaurant, we strolled around, looking in the shop windows. The brooms, leather goods, candles, and apple-head dolls filled the air with a delicious potpourri of smells.

My calf muscles began to tighten from so much walking on hilly ground, and my knees kept wanting to buckle and set me down somewhere. Our jackets became ten-pound weights on my arm. Punky had little rivers of sweat trickling down from beneath his cowboy hat.

"Let's go watch the stage show," I said.

"Yeah, D.J."

The Silver Dollar Saloon was cool and dark, and the show lasted about half an hour. When it was over, Punky said, "I'm starved."

Munching on doughnuts and sipping soft drinks, we watched wheat being ground into flour at the mill. By then, there was just enough time to visit the woodcarving shop before meeting my parents at two.

TEN

The Master Woodcarver

As we stepped inside the shop, I inhaled deeply, savoring the aroma of wood shavings and paint.

Punky walked all around a man-sized wooden Indian, trying to figure out if it was alive. I touched the Indian's face and chest, marveling that anyone could carve a chunk of wood to look like real feathers, skin, and leather.

Keeping a firm grip on Punky's hand, I headed down the first aisle. So far, I'd been careful to keep him out of the shops so he wouldn't try to swap his treasures for some of Silver Dollar City's souvenirs. Now I could almost see his mind working as he weighed what was in his lunch box against what was on the shelves.

It was easy to understand his interest. There were hundreds of intricate carvings—everything from birds in flight and trout jumping to bearded mountain men.

I steered Punky over to the counter, where the master woodcarver was giving a demonstration to an audience of a dozen or so. He had a salt-and-pepper beard and wavy gray hair. His forehead was etched with fine wrinkles, carved expertly by time, and his denim work shirt and faded overalls matched the blue of his eyes.

"You can carve with just an ordinary pocket-knife," he said, "but regardless of what kind of knife you use, it's important to have a razor edge. For that, I use an Arkansas stone."

The stone was actually two stones—one black and one gray—pressed together in a rectangular shape. The woodcarver rubbed some oil onto the black side and worked his knife across it, all the time talking in a comfortable, easy drawl. "Basswood is best for carving because there is very little grain and it doesn't split easily. Dried wood is better than green wood. The green has a rosin that dulls the blades."

The woodcarver finished sharpening the knife and went on to explain the tools of his trade. "These V-tools are for detail work, like incising lines for stop cuts. . . . This is a veiner, for carving folds in clothing. . . ."

Soon the demonstration ended, and he resumed carving a woman at a spinning wheel.

Some of the watchers moved on, and Punky started chewing on his fingers. I stayed glued to the spot.

What fascinated me most were the hands of the craftsman himself. Before my eyes, those hands used instruments like a surgeon to create a worn-out expression on the woman's face and a wisp of hair across her cheek.

Suddenly, from across the room, I heard Punky cry out, "My box!"

I spun around and saw Punky and a clerk in a tug-of-war over the Jellybean lunch box. Instantly, I knew that Punky had made a switch, and my face flushed with shame that I hadn't watched him more closely.

I shot across the room, babbling excuses to the clerk. ". . . didn't mean to steal . . . money . . . doesn't understand."

The clerk let go of the box. Plucking at the neckline of her calico dress, she glanced from me to Punky in confusion.

I flipped open the lunch box, my eyes burning so that I could barely see the three clowns inside. The two I had carved looked pitiful and plain next to a beautiful rodeo clown that didn't belong to Punky. With trembling hands, I picked up the rodeo clown and thrust it at the clerk.

"Clowns—Punky—my uncle—traded," I stammered.

The woman didn't answer.

When I spied Punky's new red socks on a shelf behind her, I snatched them up and said, "See, Punky didn't steal the clown. He left you these in trade."

"Mighty fancy socks, if they're worth twenty-five dollars," declared a voice, and I whirled around and stared into the smirking face of a fat man in Bermuda shorts. Behind him stood a gawking crowd of tourists.

"You call it trading. I call it stealing," the man said.

"You're a fat boy," said Punky, jabbing a knobby finger at his potbelly.

"Get your slobbery hands off me!" ordered the man. His nostrils flared with rage, and he backed away as if Punky were poison.

The crowd parted for a moment to let the woodcarver through, then clustered together again like vultures. I stared in alarm at the knife in the woodcarver's hand as he drew closer and closer.

Stepping up beside me, he turned around and spoke to the crowd. "Thanks, folks, for your concern, but I'll handle this," he said as he folded the knife and stuck it in his pocket. Before I knew what was happening, he ushered Punky and me into an office and closed the door.

"Sit down," he said.

I sat, pulling Punky down beside me and wondering what it was like to be arrested.

"My name's Walt—Whittlin' Walt," said the woodcarver as he perched on the desk. "What's yours?"

I felt uneasy that the man didn't seem angry. Was he playing games with me? "Delrita Jensen," I mumbled, unable to meet his faded blue eyes. "And this is my uncle, Punky—Richard Holloway."

"Want to tell me what happened?"

I told him that Punky didn't understand about money, and started to show him the treasures in the lunch box.

"My box. Hands off," said Punky, but he showed Walt the clowns himself.

"So you're a man who loves clowns," said Walt.

"Yeah, buddy."

"And who carved this one?"

"D.J.," Punky replied, plucking the clown from Walt and dropping it back in his lunch box.

"I did," I admitted. Why didn't he just call the security guard and get it over with?

"A clown lover and a whittler," said Walt, glancing from me to Punky and back again.

I started jabbering nervously under his gaze. "I've been carving for two years, ever since I watched you carve a trumpeter swan. I've tried and tried to do one like it, but I never can get it right."

"Nobody starts out being a master. The question is, do you have what it takes to be one?" Walt reached into a drawer, pulled out a gnarled tree root, and thumped it down on the desk. "What do you see?"

I felt a little quiver of fear at the odd question. Should I grab Punky and try to make a run for it?

"Well, what do you see?"

I saw a root, but I was pretty sure that wasn't the right answer, so I stayed quiet.

Walt turned the root over in his hands. "When I found this, it was just an old elm root. A couple of days later, I saw a critter in it, just waiting to be carved."

A light came on in my head. "Oh, I see. It's a fox."

Walt smiled. "The average person sees only what's in front of him. The artist sees things that aren't there."

I realized Walt had called me an artist, but the clock on his wall said it was five minutes past two. "Can we go now?" I asked cautiously. "My folks will be worried."

"Not yet," said Walt. "We haven't solved the problem of the rodeo clown. Wait here."

Uh-oh, I thought. He's been stringing us along. He'll be back in a minute with the security guard, and we'll be in big trouble.

But Walt came back alone, with Punky's socks tucked in the bib of his overalls. Giving the rodeo clown to Punky, he said, "You're a man who loves clowns, and it so happens I'm a man who loves red socks. Just this once, I'm willing to make a trade. Shake, and we've got a bargain."

As Punky shook hands with him, I dug into my jeans pocket and pulled out what cash I had left. It wasn't much—just seven dollars—but I offered it to Walt.

"No, thanks," he said, waving the bills away. "It wouldn't be right for me to take your money after we've already closed the deal. You all just go on about your business, but Punky, don't pick up any more treasures, okay?"

"Yeah, buddy."

By the time Punky and I reached the general store, it was a quarter past two. I hurried him through the store, but my parents were nowhere in sight. That was odd. Dad was seldom late for anything. Maybe they had already been here and left, and were out looking for us now.

I decided to do what Mom had always said I should do if I got lost—sit down and wait until she found me. Sitting down sounded like a good idea anyway. My legs felt as if I'd worn them off at the ankle, and Punky's short legs had to be tireder than mine.

We went across to the gazebo and found some empty benches in the shade. I chose a seat where I could see the whole main street and the door of the general store.

Members of a band came to the stage and began tuning their instruments, and people straggled in to enjoy the show. Punky sat contentedly, playing with his rodeo clown. Except for checking my watch every couple of minutes, I didn't take my eyes off the general store for fear I'd miss my parents again. I memorized every crack in every plank on that store, and I was beginning to hate the looks of it.

The show ended, the audience left, and a new crowd drifted over to claim seats for the next event. Still there was no sign of Mom and Dad.

It was after three, and I was worried. Even if the

trailer was loaded with furniture, it couldn't possibly take them an hour to travel nine miles.

I tried to imagine what could have caused my parents' delay. Maybe they were waiting for another roll-top desk to come up for sale. Maybe they'd had engine trouble or a flat tire.

By four-thirty, I was downright scared, and Punky had practically chewed his fingers down to the bone. I allowed myself to feel anger toward my parents, to mask the panic that was building in my chest.

"I'm starved," announced Punky.

The only food places within sight of the general store were the ice cream parlor and a little hut where funnel cakes were being fried.

"What do you want—ice cream or a funnel cake?"

"Big Mac."

"We can't get a Big Mac. We can't get any kind of hamburger right now. How about a strawberry cone?"

"Big Mac."

"Please, Punky, have some ice cream for now, and just as soon as I can, I'll get you a Big Mac."

"Oh, all right," he agreed, holding up two fingers. "Two dips."

I was tempted to leave him alone just long enough for me to get the ice cream, but I decided not to chance it. He might try to follow me and get lost, and *then* what would I do?

We bought two cones and went back to the gazebo. Our bench was taken, so we sat down on the grass.

When Punky finished his ice cream, he said, "I'm tired, D.J. Go home."

"I know," I replied, absently stroking the back of his neck.

"Want Shirley and Sam."

"Me, too."

"Go home—now."

"We can't, Punky. We can't go home without Mom and Dad."

Punky burst into tears. "I'm sick, D.J.," he howled, and I couldn't tell if he was really sick or if he was just trying to scare me into taking him home.

"Where does it hurt?" I asked, touching his forehead. It felt hot, and beads of sweat had formed across his upper lip. He was trembling, and when I laid my head against his chest to listen to his heart, I thought it was thumping much too fast.

I jumped up, rammed my hands into my pocket, and retrieved the bottle of nitroglycerin. I shook out a pill and placed it under Punky's tongue, and tried to decide whether to yell for help.

In a moment, Punky grinned wickedly and asked, "Go home now?" and I knew he'd played a trick on me.

"You rascal," I cried, but I hugged him anyway.

Punky's faking convinced me that we couldn't wait here any longer. He was exhausted, and that could bring on a real spell with his heart. I had to do something, but what? Who could I turn to for help?

Whittlin' Walt.

I coaxed Punky off the grass, and we trudged over to the woodcarving shop.

Walt listened to my story and scratched his head. He wrote down my parents' names, the name of the auction arena, and the description of our car and trailer. He even asked about other relatives and wrote down Uncle Bert's phone number. Finally, he suggested we wait in the office while he made some phone calls.

After about fifteen minutes, Walt came back. As soon as I saw him, I knew something dreadful had happened. Every crease on his forehead seemed deeper, and his eyes were clouded with pain. I wanted to put my hands over my ears to block out whatever it was he would say.

"Delrita," he croaked, stopping to clear his throat, "there's been an accident. The trailer—it jack-knifed." His voice dropped to a whisper as he said, "Your folks—"

I leaped to my feet. "They'll be all right, won't they? They're just banged up, and the car won't run." I laughed hysterically. "Dad's been wanting a new car, and now he'll get one and—"

"Delrita," said Walt, placing both his hands on my shoulders and gently pushing me back into the chair, "your folks were killed. Instantly."

ELEVEN

Going Home

The words were a lightning bolt, surging through my body.

Walt touched me, but I jerked away from him. Time stopped for me. I was falling through a deep, black hole, where screaming sirens wailed and faded and wailed again.

Punky's terrified voice dragged me out of the pit. "D.J.! D.J.!"

The wailing ceased, and only then did I realize there were no sirens. The screaming came from me.

Punky was gripping both my hands, his pale face deathly white. Deathly white. His heart. The pills.

I heaved myself out of the chair and fumbled for the nitroglycerin. My hands were shaking so much that I couldn't undo the cap. It was just as well. Punky's coloring had already improved.

Walt was watching me, wringing his hands.

I wanted to kick a hole in the wall. I wanted to

throw a chair through the window. I wanted to run into the shop and stomp all the carvings to splinters.

The blood was pounding in my ears so hard that . . . Blood. My parents' blood. My stomach heaved, and I pressed my hand across my mouth to keep from throwing up.

Understanding none of the situation but seeing my distress, Punky stroked my arm and said, "I love you, D.J. You love me?"

I thought my heart would break as I gathered him into my arms and wept. Punky was all I had left of home, and I clung fiercely to him, for fear that he, too, might die and leave me all alone.

"Don't cry, D.J. Don't cry," he soothed as tears streamed down his own cheeks.

Shudders wracked my body, and my teeth chattered violently. Finally I had no tears left—only hiccups and a creeping numbness.

When Walt handed me some tissues, I blew my nose, then held a clean tissue for Punky. "Blow," I said automatically, and he did.

It struck me then that Punky needed me to be strong, to see us through, to get us back to Tangle Nook somehow.

Walt tried talking to me again, but he didn't try to touch me. I hoped he understood why I'd jerked away from him before, because I was just too tired to tell him.

"The highway patrol told me there'd been a wreck on Route 76," he said softly. "I called your Uncle Bert's house and found out it was your folks. I offered to drive you and Punky home, but Mrs. Holloway said her husband is already on his way."

"Queen Esther."

"I beg your pardon," said Walt, glancing at me sharply as if I'd lost my mind.

"Mrs. Holloway is Queen Esther. Aunt Queenie."

"Oh."

There was silence for a moment, until Walt looked at his watch and said, "It'll be another couple of hours before your uncle gets here. I'll take you to my house in Branson and call the highway patrol again. They can tell him where to find you."

"Thanks," I mumbled.

"I've got kids and grandkids. If they were in a spot like you are, I'd hope somebody would help them. . . . Are you all hungry?"

The thought of food made my stomach churn, but Punky said, "I'm starved."

"Where would you like to eat?"

"McDonald's! Big Mac!"

"Come on, then," replied Walt. "My treat."

The numbness oozed out of me as I left Silver Dollar City. A thousand years had passed in one day, and I felt older than dirt. Oh, how I yearned to roll back the clock just a measly twenty-four hours, to stop my world from turning upside down.

Punky made himself at home in Walt's house. He pulled a footstool over until it was touching the TV set, and sat rolling his crayon pieces and playing with his clowns.

Even with my jacket buttoned up to my neck, I couldn't get warm as I waited for Uncle Bert. When his car pulled in behind a police escort, I pried myself out of the chair.

It was like watching a scene on TV—the police car driving away, Walt going to the door, Uncle Bert stooped and unsteady as if he were a hundred years old. His eyes were red and watery, and he had forgotten his toupee.

"Bald head," Punky greeted him, getting up stiffly and going to his brother.

Without speaking, Uncle Bert hugged Punky and reached for me. I couldn't hug back. It was all I could do to stand up.

Walt shrugged off Uncle Bert's thanks and walked with us to the car. Squeezing my arm, he said softly, "Delrita, life has dealt you a terrible blow, but you'll get through it." He handed me a small package wrapped in brown paper and tied with string. "This won't mean much to you right now," he said, "but maybe someday it will."

"Thanks," I mumbled, stuffing the package into the pocket of my jeans jacket.

"Queenie sent along pillows and blankets, so you could rest on the way home," said Uncle Bert, helping Punky into the front seat and fastening his safety belt. "Fasten yours, too, Delrita," he said.

I obeyed, thinking dully that seat belts hadn't saved my parents.

During the first few miles, Punky talked about what we'd seen at Silver Dollar City. Then he drew his feet up onto the seat and fell asleep with his head on the pillow in his lap.

I gathered my blanket around me and shivered in the backseat, not from the cold but from electrified nerves.

The ride seemed endless. Uncle Bert tried now and then to make conversation, but his voice kept cracking and he wasn't able to finish what he started.

I dozed off for a few minutes—long enough to see my parents' car smashing through a guardrail and rolling end over end into a chasm of death. I awoke with a screech that caused Uncle Bert to jump at the steering wheel and Punky to stir in his sleep. From then on, I didn't dare close my eyes.

Not until we reached Tangle Nook and Uncle Bert turned right instead of left did it occur to me that Punky and I wouldn't be going home. The realization was like having a knife twisted in my chest. I had never spent the night away from my parents, and except for the two times when Punky was hospitalized, he hadn't, either. Even then, the nurses had had to hide his trousers to keep him from getting out of bed and walking home.

Uncle Bert's large split-level house was as brightly lit as a hotel, and I fought back nausea at the thought of sleeping there.

A ghostly figure ran out to meet us. It was Aunt Queenie in her nightclothes—no makeup, hair flying loose—clucking like a sympathetic hen.

When Uncle Bert picked up Punky instead of waking him, Aunt Queenie said, "I declare, Bert, he's too heavy for that," and hurried ahead to open the door.

I drew a deep breath and followed them inside. As bad as I hated to stay here, I couldn't leave Punky alone.

Uncle Bert put Punky to bed with his clothes on, against Aunt Queenie's objections. She'd brought pajamas, clean clothes, and toothbrushes from our house.

Her eyes were full of questions, so I grabbed the bag and escaped into the bathroom. I was shocked to see my reflection in the mirror. My eyes were bloodshot, and my long brown hair was matted, the bangs on my forehead greasy.

I turned the shower on hot, wanting the scalding needles of water to ease the hurt in my chest. They didn't. They only made the bed feel colder when I left the bathroom and slipped between satin sheets.

Satin. Cold. Casket. I scrambled out of bed, ripped off the coverlet and wrapped it around me, and lay on the carpeted floor.

I drifted into a fitful sleep, only to be awakened in the wee hours of the morning by Punky, who turned on the light and came sobbing across the room. "My home," he said.

It took a moment for my eyes to adjust and for me to realize where I was and why. Drawing a ragged breath, I tried to make Punky understand. "We can't go home. There's—there's nobody there."

"My home, D.J. My bed." His almond-shaped eyes were round with anxiety, and his face was dirty.

"I know. I want to go home, too, but we can't."

"Want Shirley, Sam, my bed."

"I know, Punky. I know." The tears were building in my own throat, and I swallowed hard.

Punky lay down across my feet. "Please, D.J.," he begged. "My home. *Please.*"

I couldn't stand it. Freeing my feet, I got up and said, "Okay, but you'll have to be quiet, or we'll wake Uncle Bert."

I pulled on a pair of jeans under my nightshirt, picked up my shoes, and started down the dark hall. We sneaked into Punky's room for his shoes, then through the house and out the back door.

It was probably two miles from Uncle Bert's place to our house. Alone, I could have covered them in half an hour, but with Punky already worn-out from the long day at Silver Dollar City, every step was a chore.

Tangle Nook was eerie, deserted, and I found myself pulling Punky from streetlight to streetlight, avoiding the shadows.

I prayed that no one would bother us, because I didn't see how we could run. When I spotted a patrol car, we hid behind a shed, but it made me feel safer to know the police were on the prowl.

I turned onto Magnolia Street to stay away from the highway, away from McDonald's and any other businesses that might be open all night.

Punky was wheezing and wearing down fast, and

I remembered I'd left his nitroglycerin in the pocket of my dirty jeans. I remembered something else, too, which would be a disaster if Punky thought of it. We'd left his lunch box in Uncle Bert's car.

The Shackleford house looked even shabbier in the dark, its broken porch rails gapping like missing teeth. I felt a choking anger that my father—a good, loving, *honest* man—was dead, while Avanelle's father was in jail for committing some terrible crime. I wanted to scream "It's not fair!" for all the world to hear, but I trudged on, coaxing Punky, who was getting slower with every step.

At last we reached the house, but I didn't have a key. I had to climb on a lawn chair and crawl through the bathroom window so I could unlock the front door for Punky.

In the bathroom, Dad's shaving kit lay open on the sink, next to Mom's hairbrush, tangled with strands of dark, almost curly hair. A wave of dizziness swept over me, and I gripped the door to keep from falling.

I must have stood there for a long time. Eventually, Punky's voice penetrated my despair, and I staggered through the house and let him in.

After Punky was settled in clean pajamas in his own bed, I went down the hall and into my parents' room. The digital clock on the nightstand winked away the seconds while my mind replayed little incidents from the past. I saw Mom catapulting onto the bed, screaming that she'd seen a mouse. I saw Dad jabbing a broom underneath the bed and beating a bouncy ball senseless.

In the corner was Grandma's rocking chair, its seat and arms worn slick with use. I closed my eyes and felt Mom's arms around my small, feverish body as she rocked me to and fro.

Hanging from one burnished brass knob of the highboy was the God's eye I'd made in second grade by weaving green and black yarn geometrically around a cross of Popsicle sticks.

"Let's hang it here on the highboy," Mom had said. "It'll be the first thing I see every morning, and the last thing I see every night—a reminder that God is always watching over us."

I removed the God's eye and clutched it to my chest. Then I fell backward across my parents' bed and cried myself to sleep.

"Delrita! Delrita! You had me worried sick!"

I forced one eye open and peered up into the haggard face of Uncle Bert.

"Come on, hon, you can't stay here," he said.

I was shivering, curled up in a ball, vaguely aware of a pain in my chest. I looked down and saw that I was stabbing myself with the God's eye.

Suddenly I felt smothered by cold, harsh reality, and I shot upright.

"You can't stay here," Uncle Bert said again. His voice sounded hollow, like he was speaking from a tunnel.

"I have to stay," I insisted. "It's my home—and Punky's."

"Your home will be with Queenie and me now," Uncle Bert said. "Shirley and Sam—" He stopped as his voice caught in his throat. "Shirley and Sam had papers naming me legal guardian."

Legal guardian. The words hit me like a rock between the eyes. I didn't want a legal guardian. I wanted Mom and Dad.

"Couldn't we live here?" I pleaded, hearing the panic in my voice. And then I remembered what Aunt Queenie thought of antiques—that they were dark and ugly and depressing. If she moved in here, she'd get rid of the old furniture and replace it with fancy, modern pieces. It wouldn't be a home at all, but a showcase. I smoothed the covers on the bed and straightened the doily on the washstand. Pineapple lace. Mom was crazy about pineapple lace.

Uncle Bert's voice intruded on my thoughts. I stared at him, barely hearing the words: "If you'll gather up enough things to last you and Punky for a few days, I'll come back later for the rest."

I was a robot, doing what he asked while he got Punky up and dressed.

TWELVE

The Blank Wall

Uncle Bert's house quickly filled up with relatives waiting for the funeral. Dad's side of the family stayed at a motel, but they spent a lot of time at the house.

The whole experience was a nightmare. For the first time, I *wanted* to be invisible, but the relatives wouldn't let me. So I became a blank wall instead, sitting with the family because it was expected of me, but doing nothing except take up space.

With each new batch of relatives came the same old phrases: "Your folks didn't suffer. . . . They lived a good, happy life. . . . At least they went together. So many times, one is left to grieve alone. . . ."

I knew people just wanted to be kind, but those were stupid things to say. How did they know my parents didn't suffer? The seconds waiting to die would have been an eternity as the car hurtled over a cliff. No matter that Mom and Dad had lived happy lives, their lives weren't long enough. And it would have been something to have even one parent left over.

Aunt Queenie checked out the clothes in my closet and insisted that I needed a new dress appropriate for a funeral. "All I saw was *green,*" she said to my Aunt Donna.

They wanted to take me shopping, but I wouldn't go. I just said, "It doesn't matter. Buy what you want." After all, a blank wall would look good in anything.

Punky was the glue that held me together. With all the people coming and going, he thought it was a party, and was bewildered that my parents didn't arrive. At least a hundred times a day, he would ask my aunt or uncle or me, "Shirley and Sam come home?" Aunt Queenie would throw up her hands and mutter to the ceiling, "Give me strength, Lord, give me strength."

Over and over, I tried to explain to him that Mom and Dad weren't coming back, but how do you explain God's decisions when you don't understand them yourself?

Nighttime was the worst, because Punky cried when he had to go to bed in Uncle Bert's house. It helped when Uncle Bert brought the Ronald Mc-Donald poster and the punching-bag clown and all the little things that Punky loved, and set them up in his new room. Uncle Bert brought things from my room, too, including my Barbie doll case, but I didn't have the heart even to open it, much less pick up a knife and carve.

The night before the funeral, everyone went to the mortuary for visitation. When I walked into the crowded room and heard all the commotion, my blank wall almost crumbled. I was furious. How dare these people be laughing and talking so close to my parents, who would never laugh and talk again!

The funeral at least was a sober affair, with the very same people snuffling and blowing their noses. It was hard to figure out. Punky cried, too, not because he understood the occasion, but because of the organ music.

The dress Aunt Queenie bought for me was navy blue with a prim white collar and tiny flowers embroidered across the bodice and the hem. It was stiff and scratchy, but it seemed small punishment for a girl who would attend her own parents' funeral and not shed a tear.

I thought I'd be relieved when all the relatives left, but I hadn't planned far enough ahead to think what it would be like to be alone with Aunt Queenie.

She was a fanatic. The pencils in her desk drawer were all sharpened to the same length, and the foods in her cabinet were arranged alphabetically. Every morning she emerged from her bedroom like royalty, wearing a nice dress, a made-up face, and a pencil sticking out of her bun.

Holiday dinners at Aunt Queenie's house had always been too prissy to be comfortable, exactly like her personality. Every room was carpeted in a cream-colored shag that made you want to swing from the rafters to keep from making footprints.

Aunt Queenie's favorite room was the family room, and her "family" consisted of a hundred potted plants that she talked to as if they were people. The place was a jungle, with plants spewing forth from every nook and cranny. A huge philodendron on top of the TV had leaves that draped down and hid part of the screen. A dozen spider plants, suspended from the ceiling, had sprouted baby spider plants, which, I supposed, would sprout more babies and eventually take over the whole house.

Punky moved his sawed-off table into the family room, but Aunt Queenie hauled it to the garage and replaced it with one that matched her decor. Punky kept switching the tables, and she kept switching them back.

Once, when Uncle Bert jokingly suggested putting wheels on both tables to make the moving easier, Aunt Queenie practically went through the roof. But the day finally came that she admitted defeat.

"All right, Punky," she said. "You win. But that sawed-off piece of junk would be rejected by a secondhand store."

Dad had teased Aunt Queenie about being a "do-gooder," but I hadn't paid much attention until now. She was forever on the phone or on the go, working for some cause or community event. When she plucked the pencil from her hair, you could bet the blood bank, the garden club, or the United Church Women would be whipped into shape.

Aunt Queenie, of course, wasn't used to kids. It didn't take long for me to discover that Punky and I were just a broken fingernail, a thorn in her toe, a source of trouble in her organized life. She tolerated Punky's red plastic plate at her table of fine china, but she flatly refused to let him eat in front of the TV. One evening, when Punky tried to walk off with his plate, she told him to sit down and mind his manners.

"Don't want no manners," replied Punky, jutting out his lower jaw until his upper lip disappeared. He sat back down, but he wouldn't eat.

When supper was over, Punky went to the family room while I carried our dishes to the kitchen and started loading the dishwasher.

"Bert," said Aunt Queenie, "did you fill out the paperwork for Punky?"

Paperwork? Why would Punky need paperwork? I stopped clanking dishes to eavesdrop.

"Yes," replied Uncle Bert, "but there's no hurry."

"Maybe not, but it's wise to plan ahead. His application will have to be approved at Jefferson City, because the workshop receives funding from the state."

The workshop! I froze as I pictured Punky being herded into a dark, depressing warehouse by a man with a whip.

"My nerves can't take many more soap operas and soap commercials," Aunt Queenie continued, "and today I found chicken bones—*chicken bones*—behind the TV."

"That's my Punk-Man," chuckled Uncle Bert.

"It's not funny. We've had a drastic change in this household, and if you expect me to deal with it, you have to consider my feelings, too. The workshop is a valid solution."

I slammed the door on the dishwasher and marched into the dining room. Through clenched teeth, I said, "You can't do that to Punky."

Aunt Queenie rolled her eyes and spoke to me as if I were a two-year-old having a tantrum. "You don't understand, Delrita. There are supervisors there who are trained in dealing with the handicapped. They'll—"

"*You're* the one who doesn't understand!" I cried. "Mom kept him at home with good reason. You don't know what it's like out there for people who are—different. You don't realize how many kids have laughed or stared at Punky. Or how many parents have yanked their kids away as if he had some horrible disease!"

"Punky's a born comedian," said Aunt Queenie, so calmly that I wanted to shake her. The expert, Dad had said. Aunt Queenie did a little volunteer work with the handicapped, and she was the expert. I folded my arms and waited for her *expert* opinion.

Sure enough, she gave it. "He loves it when people laugh," she said. "Sure, kids are going to stare, because they're curious, and parents are going to be embarrassed at their kids. It's a natural reaction, and it's something we can change by being more open where Punky's concerned. I know how your mother handled the situation, but I also know nobody can solve a problem by pretending it doesn't exist."

"A problem? Is that how you see Punky? As a problem?"

"Of course not, but his life could be so much richer if he was involved with his peers. The sheltered workshop, Special Olympics. Why, I've been—"

"No," I said, remembering Mom's smoldering blue eyes. "No, no, no, no, no."

Aunt Queenie threw up her hands and turned to Uncle Bert.

He said, "Delrita, do you know what goes on at a sheltered workshop?"

I shrugged. I didn't know, and I didn't care.

"They have people with varying degrees of ability. Some do very simple tasks, and others who are less handicapped do harder jobs."

I could feel Uncle Bert looking at me, but I couldn't answer. No matter how pretty he tried to paint the picture, it still looked bleak to me.

"You love Punky, don't you?" asked Aunt Queenie.

I gawked at her. What kind of question was that?

"You're overprotective," she said. "You're smothering him. The best way to prove you really love him is to stand back and get out of his way."

In a roundabout way, Aunt Queenie was criticizing Mom, and I was speechless with anger.

Finally Uncle Bert said, "It's too soon, Queenie. Let's give it some time."

I went to the family room and sat beside Punky on the floor.

"Look, D.J.," he said, laughing at a commercial where a kitten was streaking through a house toward some cat food.

I smiled absentmindedly and started picking up the crayon papers that were littering the carpet. Maybe if I tried harder to keep things neat, Aunt Queenie would forget about the workshop. Maybe I could even talk Punky into giving up his table. After all, it was just a sawed-off piece of junk, and it did look out of place.

THIRTEEN

The Swan

I was getting ready for school when I heard Aunt Queenie screech, "Punky Holloway! What are you doing?"

I raced out to the hall, certain that Punky had been caught picking petunias or setting fire to a mattress.

He was hotfooting toward me with Aunt Queenie in pursuit.

"What's the matter?" I yelped.

"Gone," said Punky, darting behind me.

"Twelve dollars!" shrieked Aunt Queenie.

I spied the empty bottle in her hand. Shampoo. Punky had emptied her shampoo.

"Twelve dollars a bottle! Wasted! Down the drain!"

"Six dollars," I said meekly.

"What?"

"Six dollars. Punky only pours out half of it."

Aunt Queenie covered her eyes with her hand. Finally she looked at me and said, "You mean he does this all the time?"

I nodded. "But only the last half."

"And just what other tricks might Punky have up his sleeve that you haven't warned me about?"

"Matches," I squeaked. "Mom always hid the matches."

"Well, I declare. I just declare." Aunt Queenie turned and walked away, muttering about losing her mind.

I walked to school hunched over, clutching grief to my chest as if it were a notebook. Nine days had passed since the accident, and this would be my first day back.

As I traveled the unfamiliar path from Uncle Bert's house to Tangle Nook Junior High, the chilly October air stung my eyes and nostrils. All around me were trees in glorious shades of red, yellow, and orange, but I concentrated on the dead and dying leaves that dropped like tears before me, cluttering the sidewalk.

The route that had been so scary when Punky and I slipped away in the dark had put on a cheerful, sunshiny face. A big jack-o'-lantern grinned from a window, even though Halloween was three weeks away. Doors banged open, then closed, as children left their homes for school. I heard mothers calling out last-minute instructions, their voices mingled with snatches of music from cartoons on TV.

The farther I got from my uncle's ritzy neighborhood, the smaller and closer together the houses were, and the more kids I saw. Did the size of a house diminish in direct proportion to the number of people living there? I wondered, to keep my mind off the agonizing thoughts that were nagging at my brain.

Always before, there was home to look forward to when school was over. Now there was nothing. An empty house that Uncle Bert was putting up for sale. A thousand memories going on the auction block, just like the roll-top desk Mom had wanted.

Choking back a sob, I rammed my free hand into the pocket of my jeans jacket and discovered the package Whittlin' Walt had given me when I left his house. So much had happened I'd forgotten all about it.

I tore open the package and caught my breath. Inside, not more than three inches across, was a trumpeter swan in flight. Its neck was a graceful line no bigger around than a matchstick, and feathers lay in perfect rows across its outstretched wings.

Carefully I lifted the swan from its packing. Underneath was a note from Walt that read: "Life is like an untouched block of wood. We can carve out a beautiful niche for ourselves, or we can leave it unused and unproductive on a shelf."

I didn't know how an invisible girl would go about carving out a niche for herself, but I suddenly wanted to carve a swan. Tears welled up in my eyes as I remembered Dad cutting out the swan shapes for me on our last night together. He'd thought I could handle the outstretched wings, and I wanted to turn around right this minute and prove to myself that I could.

But Aunt Queenie would never allow me to miss more school. I put the swan back in the box and trudged on.

"Hi, Velveeta."

Without meaning to, I'd reached the Shacklefords' house on Magnolia Street. Birdie was sitting alone on the steps, her moptop tangled and her freckled cheeks rosy from the chill. She was wearing a sweater over her pajamas, but her feet were bare. Of course, she wouldn't be inside watching cartoons, because her family didn't have a TV.

"Hi, Birdie. What are you doing out here in the cold?"

"Waitin'."

"Waiting for what?"

"The baby."

"The new baby? Did your mom go to the hospital?"

"No." Birdie laughed as she picked up the whistle that dangled from her neck. "The old baby. Mama says I can't blow this 'til he wakes up."

A sudden burst of resentment gnawed at me. Birdie's father, locked away in a jail cell, had left her with nothing more to look forward to than blowing on a whistle. Why hadn't he died in place of Dad?

". . . How about you?" Birdie said.

"What?"

"I said I'm gonna be a hobo for Halloween. How about you?"

Birdie's eager upturned face made me ashamed of myself. How could I have wished her or anybody's father dead? God didn't make trade-offs. When He was ready for new souls—zap! He took the ones He wanted.

"How about you?" Birdie asked for the third time.

"I hadn't thought about it."

"You don't want to go trigger-treating?"

"No, I'm too old." The truth was, at the farm I hadn't had to worry about Halloween.

"That's what Tree says," Birdie replied, and her face took on a pout, "but he's not too old to eat my candy."

I smiled at Birdie and told her good-bye. She had taken my mind off my troubles for a little while. When I got to school, though, depression wrapped around me like a cloak.

The hallway was crawling with kids laughing and talking. It was just a routine day to them, but to me, nothing would ever be routine again.

I stared into my locker, unable to remember what class I had first hour. Then Cindi Martin smiled at me, and I spied her English book. English. As I sorted through my books to find the right one, Avanelle came up to me and said, "Hi."

"Hi," I mumbled. My chest hurt and my eyes

burned, and I didn't want to talk to her or anybody else.

Avanelle stood staring at her worn-out tennis shoes. I knew she was thinking she should say something about my parents, and I waited for the same tired words I'd heard so many times. "Your folks didn't suffer . . ." and on and on, with meaningless phrases that were supposed to lessen my grief.

Instead, she said simply, "I'm sorry about your mom and dad."

I nodded and closed my locker.

It was strange, but I wasn't invisible that day. All my teachers made a point to speak to me personally, and most said my grades were high enough that I didn't have to worry about making up work. Brad Miller offered to sharpen my pencil in English class. Cindi Martin asked me to pass her nail polish across the aisle to Debbi Blackwell. Debbi said she was going to let her hair grow out long like mine.

I didn't know how to respond to the attention, so I spent the day nodding dumbly like one of those silly little birds that bob their heads in and out of a glass of water.

Avanelle stuck with me between classes, not saying much—just taking it for granted that I expected her to be there. During lunch, she asked where Punky and I were staying, and I told her. That brought a sympathetic look. Once she sympathized with me at having to stay with Aunt Queenie. She'd seen her royal highness at church, staid and stiff as a poker.

In art, my classmates were making Indian pottery. There were mostly lopsided bowls and ashtrays, but Marla Daniels's vase was flawless, and she was painting it with geometric designs. When kids teased her about making points with the teacher, she said, "Hey, guys, it's my mom's birthday present. You want me to give her a piece of junk?"

I remembered the God's eye, now hanging above the marble vanity in my own personal bathroom at Aunt Queenie's. It looked as out of place as I felt.

Listlessly, I rolled my clay into a snake, then wound it around and around to form a bowl. I could have made a nice vase, but it wasn't worth the effort. It wouldn't match anything of Aunt Queenie's, and it would end up hidden in a closet.

After class, I went back to my locker and took a quick peek at the swan. I wanted to hold it and turn it and study its every detail, but that would have to wait until school was out. For now, I'd just have to be content with knowing it was mine.

"What's that?" asked a deep voice, causing me to jump.

I turned and saw Tree. "Oh, nothing," I said, hastily closing the lid on the box. If Tree saw the swan, he'd want to know where it came from, and I wasn't up to a casual conversation.

"We heard about . . . everything . . . at church," he said.

"I figured that." Why was it I hadn't been able to cry at the funeral, and now the tears were pushing at my eyes like a dam about to break?

"How's Punky? It must be hard—"

"It is," I said, not even waiting for him to finish the sentence. I had to get away before the dam collapsed. "I'm going to be late for PE class, and Cooper can really be a bear."

FOURTEEN

The Tree Breaks Through the Rock

I shot out of the building when the last bell rang. Two boys were taking down the flag, and I immediately thought of Punky. What kind of day had he had with Aunt Queenie? I was sure it would rank right up there with having his teeth pulled or losing his cowboy hat.

Avanelle caught up to me as I detoured behind the buses. "We can walk together if you want," she said. "Your, uh, new home is right on my way."

"It's not my home. It's just a stopping-off place until I'm old enough to move out."

The words sounded hateful, but Avanelle understood. My vision blurred when she switched her books to her right arm and linked her other with mine.

"How's Punky?" she asked after a while.

"He's getting by, same as me," I said, snuffling.

"I miss my dad a lot. He had to go away for a

while, but at least I know he's coming back. I can't imagine what it's like for you and Punky.''

Her voice was soft and full of concern, and suddenly I thought of that tree I'd seen growing from the rock. Just as surely as the tree needed water and sunshine to survive, I needed to reach out to Avanelle. I needed her for a . . . friend.

"I want to show you something," I said, taking the swan box from my pocket. Gently, I removed the swan and handed it to Avanelle.

"Oooh, it's gorgeous, and it looks real enough to take off and fly. Where'd you get it?"

"From the woodcarver at Silver Dollar City."

"Expensive, I'll bet."

I swallowed hard and said, "It cost me my parents."

"What?"

Words gushed out of me then as I told Avanelle everything. The terrible wait for my parents at Silver Dollar City. Whittlin' Walt. Running away with Punky in the middle of the night. The funeral and Aunt Queenie's shampoo and the horn bones behind the TV.

When I was finished, we were laughing and crying, and I felt clean from the inside out.

We had reached Avanelle's house, and she took my arm and pulled me up the steps. This time she didn't act embarrassed, and I knew why. Her home was the exact opposite of Aunt Queenie's.

As Avanelle yanked open the potbellied screen door, the spool handle came off in her hand. "Aunt

Queenie," she squealed, "put that in your pipe and smoke it!"

We burst into hysterics at the thought of Aunt Queenie smoking a pipe. By the time we simmered down, we were surrounded by grinning moptops in the living room and the aroma of hot grease and cinnamon.

"Velveeta," said Birdie, "what's so funny?" Her mouth was ringed with sugar crystals, and she held a doughnut in each hand.

"My Aunt Queenie."

"The lady with the bird nest on her head."

"Birdie! That's no way to talk!" said Mrs. Shackleford, trying hard to look stern. "What are you doing with those doughnuts in the living room? They belong in the kitchen."

"They belong in my stomach," said Avanelle. "Come on, Delrita. Mom makes the best doughnuts you ever tasted."

As Avanelle poured milk for us into mismatched glasses, I glanced around the kitchen. Flour dusted the counter and Mrs. Shackleford's belly, and the sink was piled high with dirty dishes. There was no mixer or dishwasher or microwave oven, but there was a coziness, a warmth, that made me go limp with longing.

"Delrita, wake up," said Avanelle, snapping her fingers in my face. "You're a million miles away."

"I'm sorry. I was thinking how nice it is here, not at all like Aunt Queenie's."

"Nice?"

"Yeah. Like home. Nice clutter, nice people."

"Your aunt and uncle are nice people," said Mrs. Shackleford. "Bert helped us find this place to rent, and Queenie's very active in the community."

"I know, but they got stuck with Punky and me, and they—they don't really need anybody but themselves."

"Maybe you've just had too much togetherness all at once. It'll get better when you get used to each other." Mrs. Shackleford passed me a doughnut. "Why don't you come over Saturday afternoon—you and Punky? Give yourselves and your aunt and uncle a break. Punky'd have a good time playing with the kids, and you and Avanelle could do whatever you like."

It sounded wonderful. I ate three doughnuts and listened to Birdie telling about the "old" baby chasing a cat down the street.

"I blowed my whistle—like this." Birdie lifted the whistle to her sugary mouth, but her mother said, "Not in the house."

Birdie let the whistle fall back onto her chest and continued her story. "Anyway, the cat flew up a tree and Gordy just stood there and bawled."

"Cats don't fly." Avanelle laughed.

"This one did."

I didn't want to leave, but there wasn't a telephone so I could call Aunt Queenie. I thanked Mrs. Shackleford for the doughnuts and told everyone good-bye.

Avanelle walked me to the door. Squeezing my

hand, she said, "We're going to be the best of friends."

I felt warm inside. I'd finally burst through the rock.

The television was blaring in the family room, and Aunt Queenie was assembling a club newsletter in the kitchen. When I laid my books down beside the neat stacks of papers on the table, she gave me a tired smile and said, "How was school today, hon?"

It was the same question Mom had always asked, and somehow it didn't seem right coming from Aunt Queenie. I shrugged and replied, "I got through it."

"Are you hungry? There are carrot sticks in the refrigerator and—"

"No, thanks. I don't care much for rabbit food." I didn't tell her I was stuffed to the gills with doughnuts.

"Well, then, would you mind taking Punky for a walk or something? If I hear one more commercial, I'm going to pull my hair out."

I grinned at the image of Aunt Queenie's "bird nest" lying beside Uncle Bert's toupee on the bureau. "We'll go out to the patio," I said, touching the swan box in my pocket. "I want to carve anyway."

"Just be sure to sweep up your wood shavings. They'll look tacky if they blow all over the yard. And would you mind putting your books away? I'm using the table."

I took the books to my room, grabbed my Barbie

doll case from the closet, and went to the family room.

Punky was sitting cross-legged at the sawed-off table, lining up crayons and twisting his hair nervously. I noticed his bald spot was getting bigger.

"Hi, handsome."

"D.J.!" he cried, knocking some leaves off the philodendron as he switched off the TV and got up stiffly from the floor.

I hugged him, scooped the leaves off the carpet, and slipped them into my pocket. "Let's go outside," I said.

"Wait a minute," Punky replied, donning his cowboy hat. He put the crayons in his lunch box with the clowns and tucked his radio under his arm.

We went out to the patio, where Punky started arranging his things on the picnic table. When I opened the Barbie case, we both caught the faint whiff of new wood.

He glanced up quickly, saying, "Sam, Shirley. Come home."

My hands trembled as I picked up a roughed-out swan shape, and Dad's words echoed in my mind: *Let him spread his wings and fly.*

I was still thinking about Dad that night when I went to bed. I missed him and Mom so much that my chest ached and I couldn't sleep.

I tossed back the covers, crawled out of bed and reached for my Barbie case. Aunt Queenie wouldn't know if I carved in my bathroom, as long as I cleaned the wood shavings off the tiled floor.

Huddling on the fluffy pink toilet seat, I whittled away. As the feathers began to emerge on the swan's body, I smiled.

Herkimer. The name came to me out of the blue. "Herkimer," I whispered, knowing I'd found the perfect name for what I hoped would be a perfect swan. He'd have a long, graceful, unbroken neck and beautiful outstretched wings.

When I finished Herkimer, I'd show him to Avanelle. Maybe I'd even teach her how to carve.

FIFTEEN

Aunt Queenie's Decision

That week I lapped up Avanelle's friendship like a thirsty tree soaking up water.

I found myself talking more than I had ever talked before, even to my mom, as Avanelle and I made plans. The football games, the sock hop, the fall concert were no longer events to avoid.

The one thing that bothered me was that Avanelle never told me herself that her father was in jail. In the back of my mind was the fear that since she didn't trust me enough to tell me her secret, maybe she was just sorry for me because I'd lost my mom and dad. But I tried to push those thoughts away. Whatever Avanelle's reason for being nice to me, she was a good companion.

With Aunt Queenie's permission, I began stopping at Avanelle's house after school. Mrs. Shackleford served us homemade snacks and did her best to make me feel at home. When she asked me about school, I didn't resent it the way I had with Aunt Queenie. I felt strangely at peace in that household, even with all its commotion.

On Friday, Mrs. Shackleford reissued the invitation for Punky and me to come and visit.

"Yeah," said Avanelle. "Come right after breakfast tomorrow, and we'll have the whole day."

My heart pumped a little harder. Not only would I get to spend the day, but I'd be in the same house with Tree. I hadn't seen him since I'd run away from him in the hall, but I'd thought about him at least a hundred times.

I left the Shacklefords' with a spring in my step. As I crunched through the leaves toward Uncle Bert and Aunt Queenie's, I removed my jacket and slung it over my shoulder. October had turned warm to match my mood.

Soon I spied Punky on the porch swing, holding his radio to his ear and his pretend microphone to his mouth. "No clouds," he sang. "No rain. Shirley and Sam come home. No rain."

He stopped singing when he saw me and said abruptly, "Queenie cry."

"What?"

"Queenie cry."

I took his hand and said, "Let's go see what's the matter."

"No way," he replied, pulling free.

"Well, then, you wait here while I go."

"Yeah, D.J." He settled back in the swing, trusting me to handle the situation.

I waltzed into the house, then through the living room to the kitchen, where I plunked my books on the table.

Hearing Aunt Queenie in the family room, I headed in to face her, then froze in my tracks.

She sat in the midst of a great brush pile, ranting about a pair of scissors. Mascara mixed with tears was drawing dirty streaks across her face.

The room looked terribly bare, and my arms broke out in goose bumps when I realized that Aunt Queenie's plants had been scalped. Their stalks stood tall and lonely in a hundred flower pots, their leaves, blades, blooms, and vines strewn across the carpet.

In a flash, I knew Punky was the culprit. A year before, at the farm, he'd cut all the tassels off the corn.

"Oh, Aunt Queenie," I breathed.

"My babies, my beautiful babies," she moaned, scooping up an armload of leaves and letting them fall into her lap.

I didn't know whether to laugh or cry, so the sound that came from my throat was a cross between a hiccup and a burp.

"A job," said Aunt Queenie.

"It sure is."

"No. *Punky* needs a job."

I gaped at her as if she'd said "firing squad."

Aunt Queenie got up, dusting the leaves off her skirt. She marched to the desk and snatched up the phone book.

"What are you doing?"

"I'm calling the workshop to tell them to expect Punky first thing Monday morning. Maybe they can keep him out of mischief. I can't."

My head started spinning with a picture of Punky crying for me, crying to come home. That thought stopped me cold. Punky and I didn't have a home. We were just unwanted guests in *Aunt Queenie's* home, where a bunch of worthless flowers meant more than flesh and blood.

I stumbled out to the porch swing, but Punky was gone. I found him on the patio, playing circus with Marcus Gregory. His troubles were already forgotten.

Marcus gave me a wary glance and said, "I was on my way home from Scouts when I saw Punky. He asked me to play."

"It's okay."

Marcus relaxed, but I couldn't. I felt like a wind-up toy going in crazy circles. What if Punky hated the sheltered workshop? What if outsiders couldn't understand when he tried to communicate? What if he had a heart attack?

I heard Uncle Bert's car in the driveway and dashed around the house to meet him. "Uncle Bert," I said, panting, "Punky's heart—"

He was reaching for his briefcase, and he backed out of the car so quickly that he bumped his head, knocking his toupee off center. "Is he sick?"

"Not yet. But he could be. Anytime. Especially if he's made to do something he doesn't want to do."

Uncle Bert drew a deep breath. "Are we having

this conversation because Queenie wants Punky to go to the sheltered workshop?"

"Yes, and you can't let her get away with it. He'll think we've deserted him. And who knows what can happen if we're not there to protect him?"

"Delrita," said Uncle Bert patiently, "I lived with Punky a long time before you did. In fact, when I was a boy, I clobbered more than a few guys who dared to make fun of him. But times are changing for people like Punky. They're being accepted by society, and there are opportunities now that didn't exist twenty years ago."

Uncle Bert slipped an arm across my shoulders, but I pulled away from him. He was a traitor. He had turned against his own brother.

I sat in the family room and fumed while Aunt Queenie laid out the plan for Punky's future as if he were one of her projects instead of a person.

The tension was so thick at supper that even Punky sensed it. He didn't say "Bang!" after Uncle Bert's "Amen," and he didn't eat anything except his creamed peas. After sneaking a horn bone into his pocket, he gathered up his belongings and went back out to the patio.

My eyes swam with tears as I watched him through the sliding glass doors. Carefully he arranged his most prized possessions on the picnic table. This was Punky's world—a cowboy hat, a radio, a flag, seven clowns, and a lunch box full of broken crayons. How could Aunt Queenie be so cruel as to push him out into a world full of strangers?

"I declare, Delrita, you've hardly touched a bite. A skinny little thing like you—"

Suddenly, all the sorrow and confusion and fear inside me gurgled up into a huge ball of hatred that I hurled at Aunt Queenie. "Leave me alone!" I shouted, pushing away from the table so hard that a glass tipped over and broke. "You make me sick! You have to organize everything into neat little categories—everything from clubs and flowers to corn and green beans. Ever since Punky and I came here, you've been hounding us to be perfect. Now you've got it fixed to where he'll be laughed at and miserable, just so you can be *organized*!"

My aunt and uncle stared at me openmouthed. I expected one of them to say something, but they remained silent. Aunt Queenie's face crumpled, and tears glistened on her cheeks. Uncle Bert, glancing nervously from me to Aunt Queenie, ran his hands through his toupee.

I stormed away to my room and slammed the door, hoping to knock a few pictures off the walls. Nothing happened. There was only a deafening stillness. I threw myself onto the bed, hating the slick, cold feel of the pink coverlet. Just how many heartaches could one person stand before she would shrivel up and die?

My gaze fell on Walt's swan on the dresser, and I remembered his note. How could I carve out a beautiful niche for myself in this house when I was no more welcome than a blister?

A stopping-off place, I'd told Avanelle, but that would be five long years. I rolled off the bed, picked up my Barbie case, and locked myself in the bathroom. I needed to have control of something, even if it was nothing more than a block of wood.

I slept fitfully that night. In my dreams, Punky was being tortured in a warehouse by a whip-cracking monster while Aunt Queenie yelled, "Hit him again!" and kept tabs in a notebook. I tried time and again to scream, but the sounds caught in my throat.

When I woke up, my throat felt dry and scratchy. I dragged myself out of bed and stumbled to the bathroom to take a hot shower. I was out of bath soap, so I washed with shampoo. I wouldn't ask Aunt Queenie for a bar of soap. What's more, I wouldn't ask Aunt Queenie to throw me in the river if I was on fire.

I spent a long time just standing at the closet, trying to decide what to wear. I didn't want Avanelle to think I'd dressed up for a visit to her house, yet I wanted to look nice for Tree. At last I settled on a pair of soft stone-washed jeans and a mint-green shirt that had elastic in the waist and made my chest look one size bigger than Ping-Pong balls.

As I blow-dried my hair, I pictured Mom's damp hair curling into ringlets. Mom would never have let Aunt Queenie ship Punky off to work. Wouldn't she just die if—

Instantly, a cold sweat popped out all over my body. Mom was already dead. Shaking violently, I shut off the hair dryer as my legs gave way. I sank onto the edge of the tub and sat staring at the God's eye above the mirror. I might have sat there all day if Punky hadn't come into my room, saying, "I'm starved."

When I didn't get up, he came into the bathroom and perched beside me on the tub. Taking my hand, he said gently, "I love you, D.J. You love me?"

His eyes were puffy from sleep, and his cheeks still had streaks from being pressed against the covers. He looked as soft and defenseless as the Pillsbury Dough Boy. "You bet I love you," I said, pulling myself together. "Let's see what we can find to eat."

SIXTEEN

Sitting on a Time Bomb

My aunt and uncle were gone, and Aunt Queenie had left a note telling me she'd be at the athletic field, of all places, until early afternoon.

"Probably checking all the fence posts to see if they're in line," I muttered, tossing her note aside. I knew I'd have to face her sometime, but it was a relief not to have to look at her this morning. She was bound to be mad about the fit I'd thrown the night before. Well, let her be mad. That'd make two of us.

After breakfast, I scribbled a note of my own: "Punky's with me." Feeling smug, I stuck it on the refrigerator. I'd left out the details on purpose.

I told Punky we were going visiting, which was the wrong thing to say. He took great pains shaving and perfuming himself, washragging his spiky hair, and packing his Jellybean lunch box. Finally he put on his red jacket and rammed his cowboy hat down over his ears, and we were ready to go.

We walked to Avanelle's, where Birdie, Randolph, and Eddie were waiting for us on the porch.

"Clown hair," said Punky, tousling Eddie's hair as he scooted in between Eddie and Birdie on the steps.

Eddie responded to Punky's teasing by crossing his eyes and pulling on his ears.

"You're a clown," said Punky.

Birdie giggled.

"You're a clown, too." Punky tweaked her curly mop.

Randolph hadn't said a word, but his eyes were enormous when he saw all the treasures in Punky's lunch box.

"One, two, three, four . . ." Punky counted, taking out his clowns and animals and lining them up at his feet.

"We can play pet store," squealed Birdie.

"Or zoo," said Eddie. "Let's have a zoo."

"Yeah, buddy," replied Punky.

I could see he was in good hands, so I crossed the porch and tapped on the door.

"Come in," Avanelle yelled from somewhere at the back of the house.

I found her in the kitchen, where she was up to her elbows in soapsuds.

"Pull out a chair and sit down beside it," she said with a grin. "I'll be done in a minute."

"Hi, Delrita," Mrs. Shackleford called from a bedroom, where she was dressing Gordy.

I sat down and glanced around, but there was no sign of Tree. Maybe he slept late on Saturdays.

"Do you like parades?" asked Avanelle.

Her question surprised me, and I said, "Well, uh, sure. Doesn't everybody? Why?"

"The high school's homecoming parade is this afternoon. If you want, we can take Punky and all the kids to see it."

Suddenly the cereal I'd had for breakfast rolled into a knot in my stomach. Mom and Dad had taken us to see lots of parades, but we'd always gone early enough to get a good parking spot and watch from the car. I didn't like the idea of Punky standing on the street with a mob.

"I don't know," I said, searching for an excuse. "Punky gets too excited. He might get sick." Automatically, I touched the bulge in my pocket that was Punky's bottle of nitroglycerin pills.

Avanelle pulled the plug in the sink and reached for a dish towel. "It can't be any more exciting than going to Silver Dollar—" she began. "Oh, I'm sorry. I didn't mean to—"

"It's okay." I heard peals of laughter coming from the front porch, and in that instant I knew I would take Punky to the parade. Why shouldn't he get to see it? Besides, I thought darkly, Aunt Queenie was going to throw him to the lions soon enough. At least today, I'd be there to defend him.

Avanelle led me down the hall, and I saw that there were only two bedrooms in the house and Tree wasn't in either one. I didn't have the nerve to ask where he might be.

In Avanelle's room, the two double beds were old

and sagging, but they were covered neatly with faded handmade quilts. I thought how much friendlier a quilt would be than the slick pink coverlet I had at Aunt Queenie's. Avanelle's curtains had seen better days, but they let in the sunshine as Aunt Queenie's custom-made draperies never could.

We sat down cross-legged on one of the beds, and I told Avanelle about Aunt Queenie's decision.

"Maybe it won't be so bad," she said. "I've seen a lot of handicapped people, and they seem to have a good time wherever they are."

"You've been to the workshop?"

"No, but in St. Louis I've been to their practice sessions for Special Olympics. I've helped out here a couple of times, on Saturdays. They're always needing huggers."

"Huggers?"

Avanelle laughed. "Sure. Huggers hug everybody. If it's softball, you hug anybody who gets hold of the bat. If it's track, you hug anybody who crosses the finish line, even the very last one."

I couldn't imagine Punky playing ball or running track—not Punky, whose physical activity consisted of swinging and switching channels. But I was curious about Special Olympics, so I asked, "How'd you find out about the hugging?"

"From Tree. He and some of the other guys teach the handicapped people how to shoot baskets and stuff. That's where he is now—at the athletic field."

The athletic field. Aunt Queenie's note.

"Your aunt's a hugger," said Avanelle. "Didn't you know?"

"No," I said, finding it hard to believe. Aunt Queenie struck me as somebody who would be barking out orders and keeping score.

The morning passed quickly as Avanelle and I discussed everything from rock singers to what to wear to the football game next week. Every so often I glanced out the window to check on Punky. Once, I saw him singing to a real audience of Birdie and her brothers. When he finished his song, the boys clapped and Birdie blew her whistle. Another time, I was amazed to see Punky clamp his precious cowboy hat on Randolph's head as Randolph rode the porch rail like a bucking bronco.

There were only six chairs at the Shacklefords' table, counting Gordy's high chair, so at lunchtime Avanelle and I had to stand up. I asked Punky to give her his seat, but she shook her head, saying, "I'm used to it. Tree always beats me to the chair, then tells me I can eat more standing up. Big brothers are a pain."

I pictured her and Tree fighting for the chair and grinned. It felt good to be crowded around a table with a real, honest-to-goodness family.

After lunch, Mrs. Shackleford put Gordy down for a nap and sent the rest of us off to the parade.

As we traipsed across the McDonald's parking lot, Punky said, "Look. Clown," and pointed to a poster of Ronald McDonald in the restaurant window.

"Yeah," replied Randolph. "He's coming next month."

"Here?" I asked.

"It's their anniversary celebration," said Avanelle. "He's going to put on a magic show."

By then we were at the street, which was lined with people on both sides as far as I could see.

The six of us drew a lot of stares as Punky bellied us through the crowd to a position in the front row. When he was satisfied with our location, he stuck his hand out to an old man and said, "Hi, buddy. Parade."

The old man was wearing an army coat that stretched tight across his shoulders and a cap with the VFW insignia—Veterans of Foreign Wars. Quickly he switched his cane to his left hand and shook hands with Punky. "That's right, son," he replied. "I'd be in it, too, if I didn't have a bad leg."

Someone snorted, and I looked down the row and met the eyes of a preppy-looking fellow seated on the curb. His tanned, hairy legs stuck out in the street, and he was sporting Reeboks with hot-pink half-socks. To no one in particular, but loud enough so I could hear, he said, "A general and a retard. This should be a good show."

My pulse throbbed in my ears. I was barely aware that Avanelle had grabbed my arm and was whispering, "Don't pay attention to him."

I shot the loudmouth a dirty look, and he looked back at me with an expression that was frightening.

A siren sounded in the distance, signaling that the

parade was on its way. Punky clapped his hands and chuckled, but by then the crowd's attention had shifted away from him down the street.

A police car rolled toward us slowly, its red light flashing and its siren silent. Behind the car marched four old men in military uniforms and VFW caps, their faces solemn as they escorted the Stars and Stripes.

The parade was still half a block away when Punky snatched his cowboy hat from his head and held it over his heart. As the flag inched toward us, the guy with the pink socks remained seated on the curb. Punky strode over to him, jerked a thumb upward, and said, "Up, dummy!"

Children giggled and stared while grown-ups shuffled uncomfortably. The young man gawked at Punky but didn't move.

Pointing down the street, Punky said, "The flag. Up!"

The fellow glanced around and saw that all eyes were on him. With a strangled laugh, he leaped to his feet.

"Okay, buddy," said Punky. He stepped back in place beside the "general," who winked at him, and together they snapped a salute as Old Glory passed.

"Wow!" whispered Avanelle. "That guy came off of that curb like a puppet being jerked on a string."

I nodded, feeling weak in the knees at the close call. What if the loudmouth had refused to get up? What would Punky have done then? A chill passed through me at the thought that Punky might lock horns with a scary stranger at the sheltered workshop.

We watched the Tangle Nook High School band and drill team, the floats, and the convertibles carrying the homecoming queen and her court. A tractor passed, hauling a wagon full of people wearing red sweatshirts and waving furiously.

"They're from the sheltered workshop," said Avanelle. "See their Special Olympics shirts?"

My mouth gaped open. I hadn't known there were that many handicapped people around Tangle Nook. I glanced quickly toward the preppy fellow, expecting him to call out an insult, but he had disappeared into the crowd.

After the parade, we went back to Avanelle's house, which was filled with the tantalizing smell of chocolate. As I stood at the table eating warm brownies, I wished Punky and I never had to return to Uncle Bert and Aunt Queenie's. But it was almost three o'clock, and I knew we'd better be going. I wanted us to be invited back again, so it wouldn't do to wear out our welcome.

Punky and I said our good-byes and left. Every step of the way, I dreaded having to face Aunt Queenie.

She was waiting for us as we entered the front door, her bun so ratty and lopsided that it perched on her head like an abandoned bird nest. "Where have you been?" she demanded, tearing off her sunglasses to reveal white-rimmed raccoon eyes on her windburned face.

"Kids. Play," said Punky, sidling past her on his way to the family room.

I couldn't answer. I was too shocked at seeing her in a Special Olympics sweatshirt and blue jeans.

"What kids? Where?" asked Aunt Queenie. She folded her arms and tapped her foot, which I was staring at because it was in a scruffy old tennis shoe.

"We went to the Shacklefords'," I said. "I left you a note."

"Some note! You didn't say where you were going or when you'd be back. Didn't you think that Bert and I might worry? He's driving all over town right now, searching for you and scared half to death that Punky's had a heart attack."

"I—I'm sorry," I said.

"Sorry won't get it, Delrita. I've been holding back because of all the trauma you've been through, but this is the last straw. If we're going to be responsible for you, we deserve a little consideration and respect."

By suppertime, Aunt Queenie had put on a dress and makeup and slicked her hair back into that lacquered bun.

Miss Perfect, I thought as I set the silverware on the table with the handles exactly one inch from the edge.

I managed to choke down half of a baked potato and some meatloaf before the lecture started.

"Delrita," said Aunt Queenie, "in view of your behavior last night, I believe your taking Punky and

staying gone all day was a deliberate attempt to pun-
ish Bert and me. You must have been delighted
when you came home and found us crazy with
worry."

I squirmed in my seat and didn't answer, knowing
that the note I'd left had been purposely vague.

"I'm glad you're getting to know the Shacklefords, but I refuse to let a thirteen-year-old child
rule my household," Aunt Queenie continued.
"From now on, young lady, I expect you to ask permission before you leave the house."

I could feel her eyes boring into me as I sawed
away at my meatloaf.

"Well, I declare," said Aunt Queenie to the ceiling. "This girl who had *plenty* to say last night is
using the silent treatment now."

Uncle Bert cleared his throat and said, "Speak up,
Delrita. What do you have to say for yourself?"

I looked him straight in the eye. "It doesn't make
a dime's worth of difference *what* I say. You two will
do what you want with Punky and me."

Uncle Bert folded his hands on the table and studied them. For a moment, seeing the pain in his eyes,
I thought he was going to stand up to Aunt Queenie. Then he said, "I loved my sister dearly, but now
she's gone, and it's up to Queenie and me to make
the decisions. You've grown up in Punky's shadow.
We want you to stop hiding behind him and lead a
normal life. We want him to have something that
every person needs—the feeling of self-worth."

"And the workshop will take care of all that?" I

said dryly. "Poof! Like magic, Punky's got a job, and Delrita Jensen's the most popular girl in school!"

"Well, I declare, Delrita," said Aunt Queenie. "I'd think, at your age, you'd want your own interests outside these four walls. I'd think you'd want to do things without Punky once in a while."

"The workshop is a step in that direction," said Uncle Bert. "It'll make you both a bit more independent."

"Besides that," added Aunt Queenie, "it's not like we're sending Punky away."

No, I thought, that will be the next step. Ship him off to a state hospital. Lock him up and throw away the key.

I was still upset the next day when the preacher announced from the pulpit that Punky was going to work at the sheltered workshop. At the end of the service, he prayed, "Lord, give this young man a new lease on life. Help him to find satisfaction and self-esteem in hard work. In Jesus' name. Amen."

"Bang!" said Punky, and laughter rippled through the church.

I escaped to the car, leaned my head back against the seat, and closed my eyes.

Someone tapped on the window and asked, "Need some company?" Before I could answer, Tree opened the door and slid in beside me, bringing with him the same spicy scent of my dad's after-shave.

"I take it you're not thrilled about Punky getting a job," he said.

I shook my head.

"Because you think people will make fun of him?"

"Yes."

"The ones who do will be the losers."

"Then there are a lot of losers out there," I replied.

"The real losers are the ones who don't get to know Punky at all," said Tree. He crossed his arms, and the sun glinted on their wiry red hairs. "Remember that day when he told me I had clown hair? He's so honest, it's a cinch he's not out to impress anybody. With Punky, you never have to wonder where you stand." He chuckled and added, "Avanelle told me about the guy at the parade."

"That's my point. It's like sitting on a time bomb, not knowing when he's going to offend someone or what the reaction will be. Think of all the trouble he could get into."

"But most people aren't cruel to someone who's different."

"How could you know that? You haven't been with Punky every day of your life like I have. You haven't seen what goes on."

"No," replied Tree, riveting me with his eyes, "but I know what it's like to be different. How many kids do you know who have a father in prison?"

"I—I—"

"Hadn't you wondered about my dad? Why he's never around?"

"Birdie told me weeks ago when I went to your

house to pick up the math book. I never told a soul."

Not even your own mother, nagged a voice inside me. All at once, the spicy smell became overpowering, and I heard Mom telling Dad to go easy on the after-shave. Tears sprang to my eyes, and I turned away from Tree.

"You've known all along?" he asked. "Is that why you haven't come to a game? Because I'm a jailbird's son?"

"No. I—I've always been a loner. I've never been comfortable around other people. Because of Punky." I felt sick. This was the first time I'd admitted the truth to anybody but myself.

"Sheeesh, you're just like Avanelle," Tree said, rolling his eyes. "You're both miserable because you've got something to hide. Sometimes the best way to tackle a problem is to meet it head-on. That's what I did when I came here. I told the whole football team about my dad. It was better than worrying every second that they'd find out."

"But—but—what did they do?"

"They all stared at me for a minute, then a couple of guys slapped me on the back and said, 'That's too bad, man,' and then Coach asked if we were going to have a hen party or play football."

"That's it?"

"That's it."

"Your situation doesn't compare to Punky's," I argued. "Anybody'd think twice before crossing you. You're built like a tank."

The car door swung open, and Punky said gruffly, "Hey, you, that's my girl."

Tree's eyes lit up with mischief, and he slid across the seat and threw his arm around me. "I say she's my girl."

"She's my girl, you old goat. Scram!" replied Punky, jerking his thumb westward.

Tree laughed, scooted back across the seat, and climbed out of the car. "Built like a tank, she says, but look who gets the girl."

I watched him go as Punky crawled in beside me and slammed the door. I was limp as a dish rag, and I could still feel the weight of Tree's freckled arm across my back.

When Aunt Queenie got in the front seat, she wrinkled her nose and fanned the air, saying, "I declare, Delrita, what are you wearing? It smells like a perfume factory in here."

SEVENTEEN

The Sheltered Workshop

On the day Punky was to start work, he came into the kitchen with his jogging pants pulled up almost to his armpits.

"Hey, Punk-Man, give your shirt some breathing room," Uncle Bert said as he tugged the elastic down to Punky's waist.

"My pants, you old goat."

"You're the old goat." Uncle Bert laughed.

Aunt Queenie handed Punky a shiny new grown-up's lunch box. "For your first day on the job," she said.

"You have it," replied Punky. He set his old lunch box on the counter and tapped the picture of Jellybean the Clown. "My box."

"But look here. This one's got an ice pack and a Thermos bottle."

"You have it."

"Well, I declare," said Aunt Queenie, removing

the sandwich, chips, and vegetable sticks from the new lunch box and slapping them on the counter.

I grinned as Punky calmly shuffled the treasures in his old lunch box to make room for the food. He had won this round.

After breakfast, Uncle Bert said, "Well, Punk-Man, it's time for working men to hit the road."

"Wait a minute." Punky sneaked a glance at Aunt Queenie, nestled his lunch box under his arm protectively, and sauntered off to his room. I could hear him sorting through his woodcarvings.

Uncle Bert went out and started the car. When he came back and Punky wasn't in sight, he called, "Punk-Man, time's a-wasting."

"Wait a minute."

I smiled into my napkin. Uncle Bert could drag Punky off to the workshop, but wild horses couldn't make him hurry.

Aunt Queenie poured another cup of coffee and sat down. "Delrita," she said, "Bert and I think you should go along to the workshop this morning. See for yourself that there's nothing to fear."

I jerked my head up. "But—but—what about school?"

Studying me with eyes that were made up in lavender to match her dress, my aunt said primly, "Not every lesson can be learned in a classroom."

I stood beside Uncle Bert's car, waiting for Punky to gather up his things, and watched as men and women streamed in the door of the workshop.

A huge lump formed in my throat. Some of the people were lame or had twisted features, others resembled Punky because of their Down's syndrome, and still others didn't look handicapped at all. I caught myself doing the unforgivable—staring, just like the strangers who had stared at Punky a thousand times.

Bits of conversations floated about, as if someone were flicking the dial on a television set.

"Hi, Susie. You watch Corky last night on TV?"

"Yeah. He's cute. He's my boyfwiend."

"Hey, Mike, how about those mud wrestlers?"

"I watched cowboys. John Wayne."

To my surprise, these people didn't seem the least bit unhappy. In fact, they gave the impression they were glad to be here.

A blind man moved up the sidewalk slowly, feeling his way with a long white cane. When he got closer, the lump in my throat grew larger. His forehead was caved in so far that I could have laid my fist in the groove.

"Rudy, old buddy, give me five," said a middle-aged man in a faded chambray shirt and overalls.

"Hi, Steve," the blind man replied cheerfully, reaching for the handshake. I remembered something I'd heard a long time before: Blind people "see" with their ears and hands.

When Punky removed his cowboy hat and stopped to salute the flag, I watched a driver lift a gray-haired crippled man out of a van and into a wheelchair.

"Need a hand?" asked Uncle Bert.

"No, thank you," said the crippled man, in a high, squeaky voice. With tiny hands that were twisted almost backward, he pushed a button and steered the chair up the ramp at the front door.

We followed him into the building, where a circle of employees stared at us. As I glanced around at the curious faces, I felt like a bug being studied under a microscope. With a start, I realized that Uncle Bert and I were the oddballs here, the outsiders.

The workers kept staring as they filed past the reception desk and greeted the secretary. They moved on into a lounge area, then looked back at us and whispered among themselves as they cubbyholed their coats and lunches.

The secretary didn't notice us until Punky joined the line of well-wishers and said, "Hi, pretty girl."

"Well, hello. You must be Richard Holloway."

"Punky."

Uncle Bert stepped forward. "I'm Bert Holloway, Punky's brother and guardian. I'd like to see Mr. Reese."

"Sure thing. I'll take you to his office in just a minute."

Punky was chewing on his fingers and eyeballing the flow of workers, but he hadn't offered to shake hands with anybody. What was going through his mind?

I felt a hand on my head and turned around to see a chubby man in overalls and a tan cowboy hat peering at me through thick glasses. He had doughy white skin, almond-shaped eyes, and a tongue that seemed too big for his mouth. Stroking my hair, he said, "You're pretty. My wife."

Punky puffed out his chest and bellied up to him, saying, "Hey, you old goat. That's my girl."

There was a thirty-second standoff as Punky and the fellow stood belly to belly, hat brim to hat brim.

The secretary laughed. "I see Punky has a protective nature, but Barney's harmless. He wants to marry all the girls. He's asked *me* half a dozen times."

"My girl," Punky repeated.

Barney took a step backward, removed his hat, and ran stubby fingers through his thick brown hair. He glanced from Punky to me before sprinting away and calling over his shoulder, "My wife."

"My girl, you old goat."

"My wife," countered Barney as he melted into the crowd.

I couldn't help but chuckle. Barney was amazingly like Punky, even down to having the last word.

Punky grinned, evidently deciding he'd met his match. He marched over and placed his lunch box and cowboy hat in a cubbyhole.

"Hey, that's my spot," objected a rosy-cheeked blonde in a pink sweatshirt and blue jeans. I recognized her as Susie, the girl who liked Corky on TV.

"Hi, pretty girl," said Punky, touching the pink bows in her curly hair.

Susie giggled. "What's your name?"

"Punky."

A buzzer sounded, touching off shouts of "Time to work!" as the crowd surged through some swinging doors. Susie took Punky's arm and she fell in step with the others.

"Looks like your brother has already found a friend," said the secretary.

"Shall I bring him back?" asked Uncle Bert.

"No, he'll be all right with Susie. Now, if you'll just follow me," she said, and led us down a hall to the manager's office.

"Hello, Bert," the manager said, shaking hands with my uncle.

"This is my niece, Delrita Jensen," said Uncle Bert. "Delrita, meet Charles Reese, better known as Boss."

Boss reminded me of Punky's punching-bag clown—tall and round, with a ruffle of hair around his otherwise bald head. He said, "Have a seat, young lady," and I backed into an overstuffed chair that swallowed me whole.

"Delrita's been with Punky all her life," said Uncle Bert, sitting down at my right, "and naturally she's skeptical about the workshop. Maybe you can explain it better than I."

Boss settled back in his chair and flashed me an easy grin, saying, "I like to think of this as a place for mountain climbing."

"Mountain climbing?" I said.

"Most of our employees have been kept in a valley by their disabilities. We teach them to use whatever capabilities they have to climb up to the mountain-top. They're freed by what they *can* do, instead of being restricted by what they can't."

I sat stone-faced, feeling small and insignificant as I remembered Rudy with his cane and the crippled man guiding his own wheelchair.

"We refinish furniture here, and we do jobs for factories, like packing detergent into cartons and putting ballpoint pens together," Boss said. "Sometimes it takes a lot of convincing to get a contract, but once they've tried us, they come back for more. It's easy to understand their reluctance, when you consider that society as a whole, and sometimes even the family, underestimates the handicapped."

I narrowed my eyes and looked from him to Uncle Bert. Was that last statement aimed at me?

Boss leaned forward, folded his arms across his desk and said, "Some of our employees graduate from here and go to work in the mainstream."

"The mainstream?"

"Regular jobs in regular places—factories, laundromats, restaurants. Have you heard of McJobs?"

I shook my head.

"It's a program the McDonald's Corporation has set up for the disabled, to teach them to work in its restaurants. I just sent one of my best employees over to the local McDonald's to work with a job coach."

I pictured the unlucky person learning the ropes, only to become a sideshow for every little kid who ordered a Happy Meal. It sounded like McTrouble to me.

"But we do more than just work at the sheltered workshop," Boss went on. "Our people compete in Special Olympics, which is for all handicapped people, and we train on Saturdays. Churches take turns hosting monthly birthday parties. Different clubs sponsor dances for special occasions. As a matter of fact," he said happily, "your aunt, Queen Esther Holloway, is our most active community volunteer."

Uncle Bert grinned at my look of surprise. He said, "Delrita knows how good Queenie is at organizing things."

All at once, the room seemed hot, and I felt the blood rising to my cheeks. No wonder Aunt Queenie thought she was the expert. She'd certainly done a lot more than I'd given her credit for.

"Now," said Boss, "would you like a tour of the building?"

I glanced hopefully at Uncle Bert.

"That's why we're here," he said.

As Boss led us toward the work area, I heard scratching sounds and a steady hum of voices. We rounded a corner and walked into a bright room where some workers were sanding furniture.

The noises trickled into silence as, one by one, the employees realized there were strangers in their midst. Now their sandpaper was clutched in idle hands, and dusty faces were looking toward us with curious expressions.

"How's it going?" Boss asked.

"Good, Boss," came the replies.

Barney removed a red bandana from the bib of his overalls and wiped sawdust from his glasses. After replacing them, he grinned up at me and said, "My wife."

"Barney, show this little lady what your job is."

Barney held up a wooden spindle and said, "Feel."

I touched the wood. It was smooth as velvet.

"Sand with the grain," Barney said. "Everybody sand with the grain." He pointed to the workers at his table and called them each by name. "Elaine, Martin, Freda, Ray, Connie. And Barney. Six."

Connie's face was lopsided, and her mouth didn't quite work right as she asked, "What your name?"

"Delrita."

"That nice name."

"Thank you. I like your T-shirt."

Connie looked down at her shirt and giggled. "My sister. She not know I wear it."

Boss laughed. "Connie has six sisters, and she's always wearing their clothes. One of these days, they're going to wise up and start locking their closets."

"Yeah, Boss," replied Connie, giggling again as she went back to her sanding.

The workers were relaxed now, and the noise level started up again.

"Hello, young lady. Welcome to the workshop," said an old man at my elbow.

"Hello," I replied, recognizing him as the "general" from the parade. Today, instead of a military uniform he was wearing a navy blue jacket that said "Workshop Supervisor."

Boss moved on and stopped beside another group of workers. "I've got the best fine-sanders in the state of Missouri," he said, placing a hand on the shoulder of the man with the tiny, twisted hands, "and Frankie's the best in the business."

Frankie grinned and ducked his head at the unexpected praise.

In the center of the room, workers clustered around a table spread with black plastic sheets that looked like giant photographic negatives.

"They're peeling labels off microfilm so the silver can be recycled," Boss said.

I spied Susie's pink bows, and then I spotted Punky. Seated across the table from each other, heads almost touching, he and Susie were stripping the same sheet of microfilm. The look on Punky's face was of total concentration.

Somebody poked him and pointed at Uncle Bert and me.

"D.J.! Bert!" he cried, clapping his hands with glee. "Look! My job!"

Boss strode over to him and said, "My name's Boss. Give me five."

Punky pumped the big man's hand a mile a minute.

"So you want to work for me?"

"Yeah, buddy."

"All right, then, it's a deal."

"I like Punky," said Susie. "He's cute. He's my boyfwiend."

Boss winked at me and tried to look stern as he leaned close to Punky. "I don't allow hanky-panky on company time."

Punky rubbed the manager's head as if he were polishing a doorknob. "You're a bald-head."

Laughter and shouts of "Boss has a bald head!" rippled through the room.

Boss grinned at Uncle Bert and said, "As you can see, I really crack the whip around here."

He continued the tour, and I was spellbound when I saw Rudy, standing before rows of rubber strips that had been cut from a tire. His hands moved quickly as he fastened the strips together at intervals with metal clips.

"Rudy's making mud mats," said Boss. "Even without sight, he can put them together faster than anybody else."

When I'd seen the whole workshop, I went to say good-bye to Punky.

He dismissed me with a brush of his hand, saying, "Go away. Go to school. Go to your own place."

EIGHTEEN

Alone Again

I slunk to the car like a stray cat. I wasn't completely sorry about the things I'd said to Aunt Queenie, but I wished I'd been nicer about saying them.

"Well, what do you think?" Uncle Bert asked as he eased the car out into the traffic.

"About what?" I replied, too stubborn to let on I knew exactly what he meant.

"The workshop."

"It's all right, I guess."

Uncle Bert gave me a sly grin and started whistling off-key.

I watched the mileage computer on the dashboard, its numbers flashing red and changing crazily, as if it couldn't make up its mind. I heaved a deep sigh. I'd been riding a roller coaster of emotions for so long, I was crazier than the numbers.

"It was Queenie's idea for you to visit the workshop," said Uncle Bert. "I know you two don't see eye to eye, but she's a good-hearted person and a good wife."

When I didn't answer, he went on. "What you said the other night about her being so organized—it's something I've learned to accept in ten years of marriage. You'll be a lot happier when you can accept it, too."

"I guess I was a real brat."

"Understandable, in view of what you've been through. Let me tell you a secret about Queenie. Keeping everything in tip-top shape is her way of dealing with not being able to have children. The time and energy and love she would have given a child have been directed toward her home, her flowers, and a dozen worthy causes."

I closed my eyes. That explained why Aunt Queenie was such a fussbudget, but it didn't help me feel better.

I arrived at school in the middle of fourth hour. After getting a pass from the office, I went down the hall to Avanelle's locker and took out the math book before going on to the gym. If Miss Cooper was in a halfway decent mood, maybe she'd excuse me from dressing out and I could do my homework before lunch.

As soon as I entered the gym, I saw Avanelle at the far end. She was playing volleyball, but she must have had one eye on the door, because she started waving.

I waved back as the ball sailed over the net and hit the floor at her feet.

"Way to go, turkey!" yelled Georgina Gregory, picking up the ball and tossing it angrily over the net. She might have been talking to Avanelle, but she was glaring at me.

Miss Cooper blew her whistle and called, "Gregory, watch your mouth. Shackleford, keep your eye on the ball. Jensen, bring me your pass."

When I took it to her, she glanced at it and said, "All right. Go sit down somewhere."

I climbed halfway up and sat in the bleachers, and as I opened the math book, an envelope dropped out into my lap. I picked it up and read the address:

Trezane Shackleford
165320 HU 3-A-499
Missouri Training Center for Men
P.O. Box 7
Cumberland, MO 65277

It was a letter to Avanelle's father in prison! Guiltily, I stuffed it back into the book.

I went to work, but it was impossible to convert decimals to fractions with the girls yelling and Miss Cooper blowing her whistle. I gathered up my book and papers and went to the locker room.

I was on the last problem when the bell rang. A few seconds later, the door banged open and several girls hustled in, their voices bouncing off the walls.

Among them was Georgina, dribbling the volleyball.

"We've got Michael Jordan in the girls' locker room," Sarah Ward said, laughing. She waved her arms like a basketball player and tried to steal the ball.

Georgina, showing off, started dribbling harder. Sarah couldn't get the ball with her hands, so she kicked it hard and it came hurtling across to my bench and slammed onto the math book.

The book, my papers, and Avanelle's letter went scooting across the floor.

I jumped up and made a grab for the letter, but Lori Nicholson beat me to it.

"Hey, you guys, look at this," she said. "A love letter. To Avanelle's brother."

"Give me that!" I cried, lunging for the envelope.

Lori clutched it to her chest and looked me up and down. "So you've got a crush on Trezane Shackleford."

"Please," I said, "give it back."

She turned away from me and read the address. "Hey," she yelled, "this isn't for Tree. Not unless he's in prison."

"What?" cried Georgina and Sarah at the same time.

When Lori held the letter up for them to see, I grabbed for it again and missed. She tossed it to Georgina, saying, "Air mail!"

Georgina caught the letter and looked at it. "Must

be Tree's dad." With an evil grin, she added,
"Maybe he's an ax murderer."

"Oooh, that's creepy," squealed Sarah.

The door opened and in walked Avanelle.

Georgina glanced from her to me with a smirk,
then shoved the letter at me. To Avanelle, she said,
"So your dad's a convict. Your weirdo friend here
just spilled the beans." Laughing, she and the other
girls headed for the showers.

The letter was a hot coal in my shaking hands. I
gaped at Avanelle, who stood still as a statue in a
sunbeam from the skylight. Her emerald eyes were
shooting sparks, and her orange hair was a ball of
fire.

She streaked over to me and seized the letter.
"You . . . had . . . no . . . right," she gasped.

"I didn't—"

"How *could* you, Delrita?" she demanded in a
harsh whisper. "How could you show them my
letter?"

"I—I— You're making a mistake."

"The only mistake I made was choosing you to be
my friend! That's why my dad went to prison, you
know. Because he was a friend to the wrong
person."

I blinked back tears at the look of rage on the face
of my one and only friend.

"Dad didn't rob a bank or kill somebody," she
went on in that awful, raspy whisper. "He drove his
truck to help a buddy move furniture. Only the fur-

niture didn't belong to that fellow. He was just using my dad to steal it."

"Avanelle, listen to me! I *didn't* show those girls the letter."

"So how come they got to see it? Why should I believe *you* when the judge didn't believe my dad?" Avanelle's voice broke, and she pushed past me.

Helplessly I watched her snatch up her school clothes and head for a stall.

A cloud blotted out the sun and the locker room grew dark as another swarm of girls came in to get dressed. I sat on a bench, feeling naked, even though I had on more clothes than anybody in the room.

Georgina had succeeded in scaring off Avanelle. Not in the way I'd expected, but the results were the same.

Avanelle ignored me, and I was afraid that if I forced myself on her there'd be another ugly scene. At lunch we sat at opposite ends of the cafeteria, neither of us with a tray. In math fifth hour, she sailed past me as if I were invisible.

When the bell rang after seventh hour, I went out the back door. I was embarrassed by all the lovesick couples on the low brick wall, but I drew a deep breath and plunged on past. It was either go this way or go my regular route, and it would hurt too much to see Avanelle's house and not be welcome there.

Crunching along through the leaves, I felt an overwhelming sadness. Mom had loved raking leaves, so she hadn't minded when Punky and I rolled around in her leaf stacks, scattering them to the wind.

As I reached Uncle Bert's, a van pulled in the drive and Punky got out. The sun pinpointed the thin layer of sawdust on his whiskers.

"Bye, Punky," came a chorus of voices from the van. "See you in the morning!"

"Yeah," said Punky as he tipped his cowboy hat. "See you in the morning."

All at once, an arm shot out the window, waving furiously, and I saw Barney's round face beaming at me. "My wife," he called.

"Barney!" cried Punky, shaking his fist. "She's my girl, you old goat!"

The van pulled away, but not before Barney called again, "My wife."

Punky jutted out his bottom lip, and I put my arm around him, saying, "Did Barney give you a hard time today?"

"Nope," said Punky, tucking his lunch box under his arm and heading toward the house, "he's my fwiend."

I stood still and watched him go. Punky had a vanload of new friends after one day in the outside world, and what did I have?

That night, I hid in the bathroom to carve, hoping the act would soothe me as it had so many times before.

I held the ugly blob of a snowman in one hand and Walt's perfect swan in the other. They symbolized the difference between what I was and what I wanted to be, and I had no idea how to get from one to the other.

I started working on Herkimer's wings with the V-tool, but it might as well have been a chain saw. My mind kept going back to Georgina's cruelly exposing Avanelle's secret. The situation looked hopeless. I couldn't blame Avanelle for thinking I'd stabbed her in the back. I squeezed my eyes shut, and a tear rolled down my cheek. Avanelle was my first real friend, and losing her felt a little bit like losing Mom and Dad.

I thought of Brownie, the big shepherd dog we'd had at the farm. Brownie was a good pet, playful and gentle, but he'd killed a chicken and Dad gave him away. "He's tasted blood," Dad had said, "and he'll always want more."

Well, I'd tasted Avanelle's friendship, and I wanted more.

I knew the longer I waited to talk to her, the harder it would be to make things right. But was it even possible to make things right? Would she ever talk to me again? No, I thought sadly, remembering those blazing green eyes. Her humiliation in the locker room had been complete.

My fingers slipped and I stabbed myself with the V-tool. I wiped at the blood with toilet tissue, then put Herkimer away so I wouldn't make a mess of him, too.

I'd been a loner before, and I should have been able to pick up where I'd left off, but it wasn't that easy. School was torture now.

Avanelle wasn't chummy with anyone else, but she avoided me. Once, when we came face to face in the restroom, she turned away quickly. I guess looking at me made her sick.

Every time I had to use the math book, I half expected her to sneak up behind me and accuse me of snooping in her locker. I started lurking in classrooms so I wouldn't have to face her in the hall. At the last minute, when I had to venture out, I scurried along hunched over, as if hiding a brick in my shirt.

Sunday at church it was the same story. Avanelle wouldn't look in my direction, but she took a special interest in Miss Myrtle Chambers, helping the fragile old lady up the steps and finding the pages in her hymnal.

The rest of her family was friendly, though. Birdie sat with Punky and me before going to her class, and when the service ended, Mrs. Shackleford asked me how Punky liked working.

"Okay," I said, but that was a lie. Punky was in seventh heaven at the workshop, and I'd decided he no longer needed me at all.

Tree said, "He had a great time at the athletic field yesterday. I showed him how to shoot baskets, and his aim is terrific."

No wonder, I thought, he's got the best horn-flinging arm in the country.

"You ought to come with him next time," Tree said. "We'd let you be water girl or sweep off the track."

I knew he was teasing, but the words irritated me. "No, thanks," I said. "I'm busy on Saturdays."

As soon as I could, I went to the car. A wave of homesickness washed over me when the smell of the upholstered seats reminded me of Dad's antique shop.

I watched Avanelle help Miss Myrtle to Elsie Golden's car, climb in the backseat, and ride away with them.

Soon the rest of the Shacklefords came out. Tree carried Birdie in one arm and hung on to Eddie's hand. His mother, holding Gordy, laughed when the wind caught Randolph's papers and he started chasing them.

My mind played back in slow motion the last glimpse I'd had of my parents at Silver Dollar City—Dad backing up the trailer and Mom hanging out the window and blowing kisses. More than anything, I wished they'd come walking out of the church with Punky. I ached to have a whole family again, to be like we were before the accident.

NINETEEN

Big Bucks

It rained that afternoon. Aunt Queenie drove off somewhere, Uncle Bert curled up for a nap, and I was left with Punky, who cried because I couldn't stop the rain. He sat at the dining room table twisting his hair, while I pretended to call the news three times.

The rain drizzled down, filling up Aunt Queenie's outside flower pots and washing muddy water across the patio. As I stood looking out the double doors, I had an idea.

"Punky, remember the mud mats Rudy makes?"

"Yeah," he said, wiping his face with his sleeve. "Rudy's my fwiend."

"If it didn't rain, nobody'd ever need mud mats, and he'd be out of a job. Boss would have to send him home."

Punky looked at me with puppy-dog eyes. "Rudy cry."

"He'd cry if it didn't rain, but I'll bet he's laughing now."

Punky folded his arms on the table and thought about that for a minute. Then he smiled, opened his lunch box, and started lining up his clowns.

I sat down and leafed through the Sunday paper.

In a little while, Aunt Queenie came home. She shivered as she hung her dripping jacket on the coat rack and removed the scarf from her hair. After pouring herself a cup of coffee, she sat down with Punky and me and said, "Those Shacklefords seem like nice children."

What brought that up? I wondered without saying anything.

"Tree and Avanelle are so good to help with Special Olympics. And Avanelle is looking after Miss Myrtle Chambers, who's been having fainting spells. Her mother said she spends—"

Suddenly I was suspicious. "When did you talk to Mrs. Shackleford?"

"I just came from there. I always call on new members of the church. I meant to go sooner, but—"

"What else did she say about Avanelle?"

"That she's lonely here. She doesn't fit in. Gardenia—Mrs. Shackleford—said you and Avanelle seemed to hit it off for a while, but then something went wrong."

"We had a misunderstanding at school."

"Can't you straighten it out?" asked Aunt Queenie.

"Not likely."

"But you'd have someone your own age to laugh with, to share your troubles with. Before, you had Punky, but now he's branching out on his own. Bert and I are here, of course, but you don't talk to us. You've kept everything bottled up inside since Shirley and Sam— It's not good for you."

"I'm okay."

"You've both been through the fire, so to speak. You, losing your mom and dad, and Avanelle, facing the shame of having a father in prison." Aunt Queenie chuckled at my look of astonishment. "Yes, I know about that. Gardenia confided in me. She said her husband was wrongly convicted."

And so was I, when Avanelle caught me holding that letter. I folded the newspaper and got up. It wasn't fair. If everybody already knew about Mr. Shackleford's being in prison, why had Avanelle blown up at me over something that wasn't my fault?

On Friday when I got home from school, Punky stuck a slip of paper in my face and said, "Look, D.J., my dollar."

"What's that?"

"It's his first paycheck," said Aunt Queenie cheerfully.

I took the check from Punky and saw that it was made out to Richard Holloway for forty-eight dollars. "That's not much money for two weeks' work," I said.

"Well, to him it's a fortune. He's rich as a king."

"My dollar," Punky said, removing the check from my hands and stashing it in his lunch box. Every few minutes he'd haul it out and show me again, but he wouldn't let me touch it.

I sat sipping a Coke and thinking how much he'd changed since he'd been at the workshop. His bald spot had sprouted wiry brown hair, and he'd stopped chewing on his fingers. He even went to bed earlier now, and every morning when his feet hit the floor, he was a man with a purpose.

When Uncle Bert came home, Punky met him at the door and waved the check at him, saying, "My dollar."

"Well, this calls for a celebration!" exclaimed Uncle Bert. He yelled into the kitchen, "Queenie, whatever you've got on the stove, take it off. We're going out to eat."

On the way to the restaurant, Uncle Bert stopped at the supermarket and insisted that we all go in while Punky cashed his check. "This is a big day for Punk-Man," he said, "and I want everybody to see it."

At the cashier's window, he showed Punky where to make an X on the check and signed his name for him. Sliding the check under the glass, he said, "Give it to us in ones."

The clerk, a short, plump man with a yellow shirt and plaid suspenders, squinted at the check and frowned. "Did you say ones? I haven't got that many in my drawer."

"Clean out the registers," said Uncle Bert. "We've got to have ones."

Grumbling to himself, the clerk stepped out of the office. It took several minutes for him to make change at the registers, and when he came back, he tried to count out the money to Uncle Bert.

"Not to me," said my uncle.

"My dollar," said Punky, holding out his hand.

As the clerk, looking peeved, counted the money into Punky's hand, Punky's eyes got bigger and bigger.

". . . forty-six, forty-seven, forty-eight," finished the man, rudely slapping the last dollar onto Punky's hand and turning to walk away.

Punky reached out and snapped his suspenders. "Thank you, buddy," he said. "You're fat."

We ate supper at a seafood restaurant, and afterward Uncle Bert drove to a furniture store. "Bail out," he said, and I wondered what else he had up his sleeve as we all got out of the car.

Taking Punky's hand, I followed my aunt and uncle to the television department.

"Now, Punk-Man," said Uncle Bert, rubbing his hands together, "let's pick out the one we want."

Punky didn't say a word. He was hypnotized by all the TVs running at once, and he paid no attention to the salesman who had come to talk to us.

Uncle Bert and Aunt Queenie chose a portable color TV with a remote control and a price of three hundred dollars. The salesman carried it up front.

As I dragged Punky along after them, he looked

back over his shoulder, still staring at the bank of TVs.

"Punk-Man," said Uncle Bert, "here's where you spend the big bucks. Show the man your money."

"My dollar," replied Punky, setting his lunch box on the counter and flipping open the lid to show off his pile of ones. As he lined them up on the counter, I noticed Aunt Queenie writing out a check to cover the difference.

When I checked on Punky at about nine-thirty, I found him propped up in his bed, watching television.

He pointed a stubby finger at the TV. "My show."

"You look awfully busy."

"Yeah, D.J.," he said, grinning as he punched the buttons on the little black box and changed the channel by remote control.

TWENTY

Herkimer

"Hurry," said Punky. "Play ball." It was his second Saturday to go to the athletic field to train for Special Olympics.

"I can't hurry any faster," replied Aunt Queenie, "unless you want your eggs raw."

"Clock."

"Well, I declare." Aunt Queenie pointed the spatula at Uncle Bert and said, "Two weeks ago I couldn't blast him out of bed. Today we oversleep by fifteen minutes, and he's like a cat on a hot roof."

"That's what a job and a few bucks'll do for you, isn't it, Punk-Man?" Uncle Bert laughed.

"Yeah, buddy," said Punky, lifting Uncle Bert's toupee and kissing him on the head.

"Hey, leave my hair alone, fat boy."

"You're a fat boy, you old goat," Punky replied as he plopped the toupee back in place. He gathered up his jacket, his lunch box, and his cowboy hat and set them by the door. Then he tapped Aunt Queenie on the shoulder and repeated, "Clock."

"Well, I declare," said Aunt Queenie, handing him his red plastic plate.

I sipped my orange juice and studied my aunt. I couldn't get used to seeing her in a sweatshirt and blue jeans, and I'd been totally surprised the night before when she wrote out that check.

"Delrita," she said, "why don't you come with us today?"

"No, thanks."

"Come on. Come with us. You hole up in your room so much you're turning into a mole."

How could I tell her that I liked being a mole? I was snug and safe in my room, and I enjoyed working on Herkimer. The world around me had shifted crazily, like ashes in the wind, but the little swan gave me a sense of control.

"You'd get a kick out of watching Punky," Uncle Bert said. "Running isn't his style, but he can throw a mean basketball."

"Come on, D.J. Pleeeaaaase come," said Punky. His eyes were bright with excitement, and he had egg around his mouth.

"Well, all right," I said, tousling his hair.

"Hey, rascal. Leave my hair alone."

"Oh, I forgot. You've got to look nice for Susie."

"Yeah, Susie. My girl."

The athletic field resembled an anthill, with all the ants running around in red sweatshirts. Punky jumped out of the car and hustled across the field, dragging Uncle Bert with him.

"Want to hug with me?" asked Aunt Queenie. "I'm assigned to the track."

"I think I'll watch Punky."

"Suit yourself."

Punky was clowning around with Barney near a basketball goal. When he spied me, he punched Barney on the arm and pointed at me, saying, "My girl."

"My wife."

"My girl, dummy."

"You're the dummy," said Barney, and the two collapsed in a fit of giggles.

A whistle blew and Boss yelled, "Fall in line for the free throw."

When Punky's turn came, Uncle Bert boomed, "Hit it, Punk-Man!"

Punky flashed him a thumbs-up sign. He took his own sweet time, bouncing the ball, testing it, clutching it to his chest to ponder his aim. He was hamming it up, and his eyes gleamed with the joy of it. When at last he flung the ball in a graceful arch, and sank it without touching the rim, the audience cheered.

"My fwiend," said Barney, slapping him on the back.

Punky clasped his hands over his head like a champion, then pranced over to Uncle Bert. "Give me five!"

"Good job, Punk-Man," said Uncle Bert, shaking

Punky's hand and hugging him at the same time.

I squeezed into their huddle, feeling a little glow of warmth for Punky.

"See that, D.J.?"

"Sure did. You're pretty good."

"Pretty good?" echoed Uncle Bert. "He's better than a Harlem Globetrotter!"

Barney also sank a basket, and the crowd cheered him as they had Punky.

Connie was the next player, but she missed the basket by a good two feet. Her teammates clapped her on the back anyway, saying, "Nice try."

"Yeah," said Connie. "Nice try."

I noticed Frankie alone on the sidelines, watching the free throws from his wheelchair, and I drifted over and spoke to him.

"I know you," he said in his squeaky voice.

"Yes. I came to the workshop with Punky."

"Punky's nice. He gave me a present."

"Oh? What was it?"

"A clown," replied Frankie. Slowly he reached a twisted hand into his pocket and dug out one of the clowns I'd carved.

"Delrita Velveeta," said someone behind me, and I knew immediately it was Tree. "Glad to see you could make it."

His cheeks were rosy from the cool air, and the red of his jacket made his moptop orange. "Hi, Frankie. Whatcha got there?" he asked, kneeling beside the wheelchair.

"A clown," said Frankie, handing it to him.

"Hey, that's neat. Hand-carved."

"Punky gave it to me," Frankie said.

Tree looked at me questioningly. "Does your Uncle Bert carve? He's good."

"Uncle Bert didn't do it. I did."

"*You* did? Wow! What else have you carved?"

"More clowns. Animals. I'm working on a swan."

"Does Avanelle know you can do that?"

I shook my head and stared at my tennis shoes. "No, she got mad before I had a chance to tell her."

"Girls," snorted Tree, as if it were a dirty word. He gave the clown back to Frankie, took my arm, and led me to the bleachers.

I sat down, still tingling from where his hand had touched my arm. For some reason, it was suddenly too warm, and I shrugged out of my jacket.

"You've got to understand something about Avanelle," Tree said, straddling a bleacher. "She's got a couple of real bad hang-ups—about us being on welfare, and about Dad. She's not like me. I just go with the flow. She thought it was the end of the world, being embarrassed in front of those airheaded girls."

"I didn't deliberately show them the letter. It slipped out of a book, and they grabbed it."

"I figured it had to be something like that. I told Avanelle that Birdie let the cat out of the bag about Dad a long time ago."

"And?"

"She didn't believe me. She thinks I'm holding up for you because I like you."

I felt the heat rise to my face. Was Tree trying to tell me he liked me, or did he mean that Avanelle *thought* he liked me?

Tree laughed and chucked me under the chin. "Cheer up. Avanelle's hardheaded, but she won't stay mad forever."

After Uncle Bert and Aunt Queenie went to bed, I stayed in the family room, using the encyclopedia to write a science report on frogs. At around eleven, I turned off the lights and went down the hall.

Punky was curled up in bed, sound asleep and snoring up a storm. His lunch box was hidden under the covers, and when I went over to switch off the TV set, I saw horn bones behind it.

In the bathroom, with Walt's swan as my guide, I began to work on Herkimer. My thoughts drifted away to Tree and Frankie at the athletic field. Tree was so big and healthy, and Frankie was so small and frail. I was glad Punky had given him the clown.

Slowly, the idea came to me of giving Herkimer to Avanelle. He could be my peace offering.

I was so intent on my work I didn't notice Aunt Queenie had come to the doorway.

"Delrita?" she said, and I nearly fell off the toilet seat.

"Oh, you're carving. I thought you might be sick." She looked younger in her nightgown, with her hair loose and no makeup. As she moved toward me, wood shavings clung to her fuzzy slippers.

"I'll clean up the mess," I said quickly.

Aunt Queenie tossed a stray lock of hair over her shoulder and asked, "What are you making?" She turned my swan over and over in her hands before holding him up to Walt's.

In comparison, Herkimer looked horribly imperfect, and I blurted out, "That one came from Silver Dollar City."

"Ah, yes. Whittlin' Walt, the master woodcarver." Aunt Queenie handed Herkimer back and studied my face. "You've got the makings of a master in you," she said, "but why are you hiding in the bathroom in the middle of the night?"

"Privacy, I guess, and it's easy to sweep up the shavings."

"Well, I declare. From now on, young lady, you can carve in the family room. Bert has an old tarp we'll lay down to protect the carpet. We can't have you hiding your light under a bushel."

Tears came to my eyes as I looked up at her, unable to speak.

Placing a hand on my shoulder, Aunt Queenie said gently, "Your swan reminds me of Punky. They both started out with the basic ingredients, but it took a special touch for them to spread their wings and fly."

Punky sat in front of the TV, breaking some crayons, while I sat cross-legged on the tarp, putting the finishing touches on Herkimer. I smiled to myself.

Less than a week before, I'd never have dreamed of whittling in Aunt Queenie's favorite room.

For six nights, I'd been poring over Herkimer in the family room, and I felt a little shiver of delight at knowing he was the best piece I'd ever done.

The pole lamp behind me cast just the right light, and as I brushed the little swan with a coat of walnut stain, I imagined I saw a smile in his wooden eyes. He wasn't perfect by a long shot, but still there was good detail on the feathers of his outstretched wings. His neck was graceful, not much bigger around than a matchstick and, best of all, not broken.

I knew Dad would have been proud of me. I only hoped that Herkimer would break the ice with Avanelle so we could be friends again.

Aunt Queenie came in from the dining room and stood beside me. "Delrita, that's lovely," she said, bending down for a closer look. "Bert," she called over her shoulder, "come see this."

Uncle Bert came in carrying his rolled-up newspaper. Thumping it against his leg, he teased, "You're turning into quite a little chiseler."

Not wanting to be left out, Punky got up and joined us, saying, "Pretty bird."

I looked up, feeling proud but bashful at their admiring faces.

Uncle Bert helped me fold up the tarp and put away my things. "You've got a real talent, hon," he said softly. "Wish your mom and dad could see."

"Me, too." I carried the little swan to my room, set him on the dresser, then got ready for bed. Before turning out the light, I blew a kiss at the God's eye and Herkimer—and prayed that Avanelle would understand just how much of me had gone into the gift.

Herkimer was missing when I awoke, and in his place was a handful of broken crayons. Punky! I dashed through the house, but everyone had already gone to the athletic field.

I threw on some clothes, and sneakers without socks, and grabbed my jacket. Brushing my hair on the run, I jogged across town to the athletic field.

Punky was in line to shoot baskets, and when he saw me, he grinned and called, "Hi, pretty girl. Play ball?"

"Not now," I said, panting. "Where's your lunch box?"

"Susie," he replied, pointing in the general direction.

I ran off, shading my eyes as I scanned the runners on the track. The big red bows in Susie's blond hair singled her out from the other runners, and I dashed to the finish line to catch her. Boss and Aunt Queenie were cheering everybody, but I kept my eyes on Susie.

A few yards from the home stretch, she stumbled and fell, raking her palms across the cinders.

Boss ran and helped her up, but when she looked at her bloody hands, she burst into tears. "I'm going to heaven, Boss! I'm going to heaven!"

"No, no, you'll be fine."

"Oh, I'm going to heaven!" she wailed at the sky.

"Susie," shouted Boss, "you're going to heaven, but not *today*."

"Not today?"

"Not today."

The tears stopped, as if by magic, and Boss guided Susie to a bench where there was a first-aid kit, and began to clean her wounds.

When he was finished, Susie stood up and headed straight for Frankie, who was sitting on the sidelines in his wheelchair, guarding Punky's lunch box in his lap.

Susie reached into the lunch box, picked up Herkimer, and said, "Look, Frankie. See my pretty bird? Punky gave him to me. I like Punky. He's my boyfwiend."

My heart sank. Herkimer was just as gone as if he'd soared over the rooftops.

TWENTY-ONE

The Rock

I was going into school by the back way when I saw Tree perched on the wall with Cindi Martin. Cindi had one of those new, crinkly permanents in her long sandy hair, and big gold hoops dangled from her ears. The hairdo, together with her denim miniskirt and pink turtleneck sweater, made her look about sixteen.

When she laughed at something Tree said, I felt a stab of jealousy.

Tree's eyes met mine, and he said, "Delrita Velveeta, over here."

Cindi smiled at me and jumped down, saying, "I'll talk to you later, Tree."

I walked toward him, feeling awkward.

"Cindi kept the seat warm for you," Tree said, patting the wall. As I boosted myself up, he asked, "How's it going?"

"Okay."

"Well, you look grouchier than Avanelle, and she's been growling around the house like an old bear. Why don't you two try to patch things up?"

I picked at my fingernails and tried to ignore Wanda McGee and the boy next to us, who were kissing. Was it possible that Avanelle was as unhappy as I?

"Cool it, Mike," Tree warned when he saw my PE teacher. "Cooper is on the prowl."

As the teacher breezed past and gave Wanda and Mike a dirty look, Wanda muttered under her breath, "Old maid."

"That old maid," Tree whispered in my ear, "is one of the chaperones for the sock hop."

His closeness sent a shiver sliding all the way down my backbone, and I thought I might fall off the wall.

"Want to go?" he asked, his eyes twinkling.

"What? Where?"

"The sock hop a week from Friday. Want to go with me?"

Either that wall was moving or I was, and I dug the heels of my sneakers into the bricks.

"We can go with Mike and Wanda. His mom will drive us there and back."

I just sat there, dumb as a post.

"Yes or no, or would you rather not be seen with a jailbird's son?"

I whipped around to look at him and saw that he was teasing. "Yes. I mean yes, I'll go. Not yes, I don't want to be seen with you."

"Good. We'll pick you up around seven."

★   ★   ★

Thoughts of Tree chased around in my head as I chased around looking for his sister. I had to talk to her now, before I lost my nerve. She wasn't in the hallway or her first-hour classroom, and I finally found her reading in the library. I drew a deep breath and walked over to her table. "Avanelle, I—uh—we—need to talk."

She marked her place with her finger, then looked up at me and waited.

"I'm really sorry about that day in the locker room," I said, sitting down across from her. "The letter just fell out."

She didn't say anything, and I couldn't read the look in her eyes.

I tried again. "Maybe we could—uh—do something together this afternoon. Get a Coke or something?"

"I can't. I'm going to Miss Myrtle's after school."

I stood up, feeling like a fool. Nothing had changed with Avanelle, and I certainly wasn't going to force my friendship down her throat.

After school, I flopped on the couch in the family room to watch music videos on MTV.

"Why the sudden interest in dancing?" Aunt Queenie asked after I'd lain there about an hour.

"There's a sock hop next Friday. Tree asked me to go. If that's all right with you."

"Well, I declare," she said, grinning. "If you need lessons, just ask Bert. He's another Fred Astaire."

* * *

Uncle Bert gave me a crash course in dancing, and Aunt Queenie took me shopping to buy a new outfit for the sock hop.

I pawed eagerly through the racks, for once passing over the greens for a blue that matched my eyes, and picked out a soft sweater and a swirly skirt that didn't draw attention to my pipe-cleaner legs.

On the day of the dance, I hurried home from school to shower and wash my hair. Leaning toward the mirror, curling iron in hand, I couldn't stop smiling. In fact, I'd been smiling so much lately my face hurt.

I showed up for supper in my bathrobe, but my stomach was doing flip-flops, and I couldn't eat.

At six o'clock, I put on my new clothes and let Aunt Queenie make up my face.

When she was finished, she said, "I declare, Delrita, you look beautiful," and I glowed inside, knowing she was right.

At last I was ready, and I went to the family room to wait.

Punky tried unsuccessfully to whistle and finally just said, "Pretty girl!"

"Trezane Shackleford better carry a stick to beat the boys off," said Uncle Bert.

But seven o'clock came and went without Tree. Then seven-thirty. The grandfather clock ticked away the minutes while my aunt and uncle and I waited with smile-frozen faces.

Punky knew something was wrong. He sat down

beside me and said, "I love you, D.J. You love me?"

I only nodded, afraid of the tears that were threatening to break loose. At seven forty-five, I scurried to my room so no one would see me cry.

Tree had played a cruel trick on me, to get even for Avanelle. I crawled into bed to stop the numbing coldness creeping over me. Salty tears dammed up against my nose and trickled into my mouth.

This was my fault, I thought angrily, for allowing Tree and Avanelle to get too close to me. I should have known better. I was the *rock,* cracked and crumbling, not the tree after all.

Eventually, the phone ringing in the hall disturbed my twilight zone, and I heard Aunt Queenie's muffled voice.

A moment later, she came into my room. "Delrita, honey," she said, "there's a call for you."

"Is it Tree?" I hoped fervently that he'd have a logical explanation. Maybe he'd been hit by a train or his house had burned down.

"I don't think so, but it's a boy."

I climbed out of bed and went to the phone. "Hello?"

"Delveeta," said a male voice, and my hand tensed on the receiver. Whoever this was didn't even know my correct name.

"Delveeta," he said again, too loud because of the music in the background, "is that you?"

"Yes. Who is this?"

"It's Mike. Delveeta, Tree asked me to call since he doesn't have a phone."

There was a shuffling sound and some giggling, and Mike mumbled a few words to someone else before getting back to me. The gigglers were a girl and a boy, and I was beginning to smell a rat.

"I've been trying for an hour," Mike said, "but the number in the book has been disconnected, and nobody knew where you lived."

"Then how'd you find me?"

"Old lady Cooper finally unlocked the office and looked in your file. This number was on the card."

"But where's Tree?"

"Oh, he said to tell you he had to baby-sit. . . . Look, Delveeta, Wanda's pretty ticked off. I've got to go," Mike said, and he hung up the phone.

Baby-sit. Baby-sit! I slammed down the receiver. Surely anybody who could dream up this whole scam could find a better excuse than that.

I ran back to my room and aimed for the bed. Was that Tree I'd heard giggling because Mike had mixed up "Delrita Velveeta"? I cringed, wondering just how many people were in on the joke.

Pulling the covers over my head, I curled up in a ball. I wanted to hide, like a worm in a cocoon.

Soon Aunt Queenie came in. "Was that about Tree?"

"Please don't mention that name in my presence," I said from under the covers.

"If you'd still like to go—"

"Forget it," I mumbled. No self-respecting worm would go to a school dance by herself.

* ★ ★ ★

I woke up fighting my way out of a cocoon, but it was only the swirly skirt, tangled around my legs. I yanked off the blue outfit and tossed it into the clothes hamper. I wanted to throw it in the trash.

Last night's makeup was smudged all over my face. My eyes were dark circles, and a pimple had formed on my chin. That figured. Delrita Jensen had nothing to show for her first date but two black eyes and a zit.

I climbed into my comfortable old jeans and a T-shirt and washed my face. It would be a couple of hours before anyone else was up, so I hauled my Barbie case to the family room. When I picked up another roughed-out swan, it reminded me of Dad. For a long time, I just sat and tried to figure out why God thought He needed my folks more than I did.

Pulling on my jacket, I wandered out to the patio and looked at the sky. It was a huge black dome, and I imagined Mom and Dad up there, waiting for the angels to open it, like raising the lid on a bread box.

When the eastern sky had turned pink, a light came on in the bedroom, and I realized Aunt Queenie would think I'd lost my marbles if she found me outdoors. I slipped back inside and down the hall to my room. Later, I pretended to stretch and yawn as I entered the kitchen.

Uncle Bert and Aunt Queenie gave me sympathetic looks, but they didn't bring up the subject of Tree.

Punky came in, hiking up his pants and saying, "I'm starved."

"You're always starved, High Pockets," replied Uncle Bert. He pulled Punky's elastic down a notch.

"My pants, you old goat."

"You're the old goat."

"You two better quit fooling around and eat, or we'll be late," said Aunt Queenie as she dished up the bacon and eggs.

"You heard her, Punk-Man. You don't want to miss your chance at the free throw."

Punky asked me, "Play ball?"

"Not today." Maybe never. I didn't want to have to look at Trezane Shackleford.

"We'd like you to come," said Aunt Queenie.

I pushed the eggs around on my plate and shook my head.

Aunt Queenie said, "Then how about if we pick you up afterwards for lunch at McDonald's? It's their anniversary celebration, and Ronald McDonald's coming to put on a magic show."

"Wonald McDonald! Clown!" cried Punky. "Please, D.J."

To him, seeing Ronald McDonald in person was the chance of a lifetime. How could I refuse? "Okay, handsome. I'll go."

"It's a date," said Uncle Bert. Then he clapped his hand over his mouth and mumbled, "I'm sorry."

"It's okay," I said, but I had the same awful taste in my mouth as I'd had the morning I'd mistaken Preparation H for toothpaste.

TWENTY-TWO

The Invisible Shell

At lunchtime, when my aunt and uncle came by to pick me up, Punky was in the backseat with Barney.

I climbed into the car, and Barney said, "My wife."

"My girl, you old goat," Punky answered.

They argued all the way to McDonald's, and as Uncle Bert pulled into the parking lot, Barney said, "My fwiend works here. My fwiend Pete."

"Boss told us," said Uncle Bert. "I wonder if he likes the McJobs program."

"Yeah," said Barney, pushing his glasses up on his nose. "Lots of dough."

When Punky removed his cowboy hat and saluted the flag, a man pumping gas across the street stared so hard I thought his eyes might pop out of his head.

Aunt Queenie cast him a withering glance and muttered, "Some people could use a few manners."

The restaurant was crowded and noisy, but it was

easy to spot Pete, because he had Down's syndrome. I was astounded to see him taking orders and working the cash register the same as the other employees.

"Hi, Pete," Barney called as we walked toward a booth.

Pete flashed him a million-dollar smile and went back to his customers.

Uncle Bert brought our food, and Punky started dealing out hamburgers and french fries like a card sharp. "Hurry," he said. "Clown."

"Take your time," said Aunt Queenie. "The show won't start for another half-hour."

By the time we had finished eating, most of the crowd had drifted outside to a makeshift stage in the corner of the parking lot.

"Let's go," said Barney, standing up and sucking the last bit of his drink through the straw.

"Out," said Punky as he tried to scoot Uncle Bert out of the booth.

Uncle Bert laughed and stood up, and Punky and I slid across the seat.

"You three go on and enjoy the show," Uncle Bert said. "Queenie and I'll stay here and have another cup of coffee."

Punky and Barney raced each other out the door.

I followed them across the parking lot to the stage, which held mysterious-looking props for the magic show and a giant bouquet of helium-filled balloons.

Punky and Barney bellied up close, but I stood off by myself at the edge of the crowd.

Someone bumped against me and said, "I'm sorry." It was Rudy, the blind man from the workshop. I watched, fascinated, as a vein pulsed in his caved-in forehead.

There was a burst of loud music, and Ronald McDonald stepped out of a motor home and ran up the steps to the stage. His mop of hair gleamed fire-engine red against his white-painted face, and his oversized ankle boots slapped the ground with every step.

He whipped a red bandana in the air, and it became a string of red and yellow kerchiefs. "Good afternoon, boys and girls and moms and dads," he said. "I call my show The Big Red Shoe Review because someone here is wearing big red shoes."

The crowd roared with laughter and yelled, "You are!"

"Ronald McDonald," breathed Rudy beside me. "I see Ronald McDonald."

Ronald juggled colored balls and made objects disappear in a velvet bag. He poured water from a jug that somehow never emptied. He asked a girl to hold his magic wand, but every time she took it, the wand broke.

Almost at Ronald's feet, Punky stared spellbound, clapping harder and laughing louder than anybody else except Rudy. Few people noticed him, though, because everyone's attention was centered on Ronald.

Finally, waving a huge white flag over the audience, Ronald said:

> "If I had Aladdin's lamp and I could
>   make a wish,
> I'd wish not for a Big Mac or any
>   fancy dish.
> I would not wish for money,
> But I'll tell you what I'd do.
> I'd wish to have another bunch of
>   friends
> Like you and you and you.
> Bless you, and thank you for coming
>   to my show today."

At Ronald's invitation, children started filing across the stage for handshakes and balloons. When Punky and Barney got in line, I perched on the hood of a car to wait.

As the line snaked along, I watched the people who came into view from behind a row of parked cars. Most of them were strangers, but I recognized Marcus Gregory and our preacher's three kids.

Then I saw Rudy, feeling his way carefully with his cane. At last he reached the edge of the stage and stood listening for a cue that he should move on.

Ronald posed for a picture with a little girl and sent her off with a balloon. When he saw Rudy, he said, "Hello, young fellow. My name's Ronald McDonald."

"Really?" Rudy stepped forward hesitantly. "Are you the *real* Ronald McDonald?"

"See for yourself." Ronald took Rudy's hand and ran it across his head, saying, "I've got lots of red hair. And a great big nose."

"I see Ronald McDonald!" exclaimed Rudy, jiggling with excitement.

"Are you afraid?" asked Ronald.

"No. Why?"

"You're shaking."

Rudy laughed and said, "You're funny."

"I should hope so. That's my job." As Ronald put a balloon in Rudy's hand and helped him across the stage, Rudy's face was full of wonder at what he'd seen.

I looked back to check how Punky had progressed in the line, and spied four redheads in a row—Birdie, Randolph, Eddie, and Tree! Tree was walking backward, talking to Cindi Martin, who had a little boy by the hand.

Cindi's cheeks were flushed, and her crinkly hair glistened in the sun. Tree bent down and whispered to her, and they both laughed. Something clicked in my brain as I remembered seeing them together on the wall. I knew now why they'd been laughing. Tree had stood me up to go with Cindi Martin to the sock hop!

I scrambled off the car, wanting to get away from him, but Birdie spotted me.

"Hi, Velveeta," she called. "Guess what we got."

I froze as Tree started toward me. Before I could

force my legs to move, he was saying, "I'm really sorry about last night—"

"I'll bet," I said hotly.

He looked at me with a puzzled expression. "Didn't Mike call you? He was supposed to as soon as he got to the dance. You see, it was an emer—"

"He called."

"Then why are you mad?"

"For one thing, you set me up. For another, I thought we were friends."

"We are."

I tried to laugh, but it was an ugly sound. "Del-*veeta* Jensen won't fall for your tricks again. Now quit wasting my time."

As I turned away, Tree caught my arm. "Delrita, what's the matter with you? I couldn't help—"

"Take your hands off me!" I screeched, not caring that Cindi Martin and half of Tangle Nook were staring at us. "Leave me alone! If I live to be a hundred, I never want to see your face again!" I stormed away from him and ran blindly across the parking lot.

Aunt Queenie and Uncle Bert were standing on the sidewalk, talking to Brother Hicks.

"Tell Delrita what you just told us," said Aunt Queenie.

The preacher smiled. "Gardenia Shackleford had a baby girl last night."

"That's nice," I mumbled.

"She went into labor pretty fast," said Aunt

Queenie, "and Avanelle was with Miss Myrtle Chambers. Tree had to baby-sit."

Her words chilled me to the bone. Tree *hadn't* played a trick on me. The anger I'd felt only moments before turned into pure shame. How could I have said those awful things to him? How could I undo the damage? You can't, said an inner voice. You can't turn back. You've burned your bridges.

I must have looked as miserable as I felt, because Aunt Queenie asked, "Are you all right?"

"Yeah, but I—I think I'll walk, if you don't mind. I need some fresh air."

I walked slowly, as if struggling through ankle-deep mud. I was a jinx. A weirdo. First I'd hurt Avanelle, and now Tree. I didn't deserve to have any friends. Georgina Gregory had done the world a favor by warning people about me.

I would go back to being invisible. An invisible girl couldn't have friends, but she couldn't hurt anybody, either. By the time I reached the house, I'd climbed into an invisible shell. I snuggled down inside it, determined that nothing could make me come out. Not today, not tomorrow, not ever again.

TWENTY-THREE

Heartache

I just couldn't face Tree the next day, so I pretended to be sick and missed church.

Afterward, Aunt Queenie came into my room and found me still in my pajamas, reading. "They named the baby Elmira," she said, sitting down beside me on the bed.

"Elmira, New York."

"What?"

"It's a private joke."

"Oh," said Aunt Queenie, looking puzzled. "Well, Avanelle said her mother and the baby are coming home Tuesday. I think you and I should go see them. Maybe take a gift."

"I couldn't."

"But why? Tree had a perfectly good reason for missing your date. Surely you're not mad about that."

"No," I replied. "I'm just—mixed up."

"Mixed up? About what? Can't you talk to me about it?"

"It wouldn't do any good. You see, I said some things. Hateful things."

Aunt Queenie smiled. "You did that to me not too long ago. But you know what? You were right. I *am* too organized. I'm trying hard to be a bit of a slob."

I couldn't help but laugh. "Trying hard to be a slob. Aunt Queenie, only you would think of that."

On Monday, I saw Tree coming up the hall toward me, and I did my best to hide in my locker. There was room only for my head and one shoulder, and when I came up for air, he was standing beside me with his arms folded. He looked mad.

"What's the deal, Delrita?" he asked. "What made you scream like a banshee at McDonald's and then leave me with my bare face hanging out?"

"I—uh—I—"

"*You* ran off, but I had to hang around with everybody staring at me like I had two heads."

"I'm sorry," I said, realizing just how much I'd hurt his pride. "When you didn't come Friday night, I thought you'd . . . done it on purpose."

"I wouldn't pull a stunt like that."

"I know," I said in a small voice. I felt lower than a snake.

"So what's next? Where do we go from here?" Tree's anger had passed, and he was searching my face.

I wanted to say, "Let's be friends again—pretend nothing happened," but I'd already made up my mind to be invisible. If I wasn't, I'd only end up hurting him again. I swallowed hard and said, "Nowhere. I guess we go nowhere."

A couple of days later, Miss Cooper took our class out to the softball field for PE.

The bases were loaded when I got up to bat, and naturally, with Georgina Gregory eyeing me from the shortstop position, I struck out. Ignoring the groans of my teammates, I went over to sit on the bench.

After the next batter hit a single, Avanelle ran from third to home plate. I couldn't believe it when she kept running straight toward me.

She stopped in front of me, and panting she said, "Mom said I should invite you to come and see the baby."

In my mind's eye, I saw her house with its friendly old furnishings and homey atmosphere, and I was tempted to say yes.

"I got it," yelled Georgina, and I looked up to see her snatching the next hit in her glove. "Three outs with the bases loaded," she cried gleefully to the pitcher. "They're a team full of turkeys."

Turkey. Weirdo. Jinx.

I kicked at the dust with my tennis shoe as I said to Avanelle, "I don't think so. I'd only bring bad luck."

*   *   *

From then on, all the days ran together as I moved about in my shell.

I knew Thanksgiving was coming because all the stores had put up Christmas decorations, and Aunt Queenie had made lists of who would be coming and what to cook for the family dinner. Every day she rolled out a different kind of pie and stored it in the freezer.

I went back to hiding in the bathroom so I could carve a Ronald McDonald for Punky for Christmas.

On Thanksgiving Day, the house overflowed with relatives I hadn't seen since Mom and Dad's funeral. They seemed too cheerful and asked too many questions to suit me. I even thought about writing my answers on cards and flashing the appropriate response:

A. I'm fine.
B. Yes, Punky has changed.
C. School is okay.
D. I don't want anything for Christmas.

As I helped Aunt Queenie set up card tables and lay out lace tablecloths, Punky flitted about happily, talking about a party.

At the dinner table, when my Great-uncle Raymond thanked God for the opportunity to gather together with loved ones, my eyes filled with tears.

"Lord," finished Uncle Raymond, "help us to

seek Your will for our lives. In Jesus' name we pray. Amen."

"Bang!" said Punky. "I'm starved!"

Everybody else laughed, but I excused myself to blow my nose.

The next day, we decorated the Christmas tree, and Aunt Queenie bought some poinsettias to brighten up the family room.

"Punky Holloway," she said, shaking a finger at him, "don't even *think* about pruning these flowers. Remember, Santa is coming—"

"Santy Claus, presents."

"Not if you touch my flowers."

"Ohhhh-kay, you win," said Punky, and I laughed.

Somehow, Aunt Queenie roped me in to help with the Christmas party her club was giving for the workshop in a couple of weeks.

"Take your pick," she said. "You can either serve refreshments or help with the gifts."

"I'll serve."

"Good. These parties are so much fun," she said, her eyes shining. "We always have a live band and dancing and a visit from Santa."

Her enthusiasm was catching, and before I knew it, I was in the Christmas spirit. We spent all afternoon baking cookies.

I was doing fine until the red icing triggered the memory of Mom decorating Punky's birthday cake. I laid down the icing bag and stared off into space.

Aunt Queenie came over and put her arm around me. "It's hard, isn't it, especially during the holidays? I lost my mother five years ago, and I still sometimes forget she's gone. Just last week, I saw a sweater at Penney's and thought, Mama would like this."

I nodded. It helped to know that someone understood.

"I'm tired of this mess anyway," said Aunt Queenie. "Let's clean it up, freeze the cookies, and finish decorating them another time."

"Another time" never came. On Monday afternoon, I was in science class when the secretary called for me on the intercom.

I went to the office, where I found Aunt Queenie pacing the floor, her rouge resembling spilled paint on her white cheeks. "Get your coat," she said. "I've already signed you out."

"What's the matter? Is it Punky?"

"Just get your coat. I'll wait for you outside."

Willing myself not to think, I ran to my locker, grabbed my coat, then ran to the car. Before I got the door completely closed, Aunt Queenie had us moving down the drive.

"Punky's sick," she said. "It's—it's pretty bad."

Panic rose in my throat. "How bad?"

"He might not make it this time."

"No!" I screamed. "No! He'll be all right. He's been sick before."

"Not like this."

"What—how—when?"

"At work. Boss called. Punky's on his way to Sedalia in an ambulance."

"The nitroglycerin—didn't Boss use it?"

"He used it. It just didn't do much good."

"Where's Uncle Bert?"

"With Punky."

Aunt Queenie drove like a wild woman while I hung on to the armrest and prayed that Punky wouldn't die.

Within a half-hour, we were racing down the hospital corridor toward Intensive Care.

Uncle Bert met us, his face ashen. "We can't go in yet," he said. "We're allowed ten minutes every hour, two visitors at a time. I just came out."

"How is he?" I croaked.

Uncle Bert's face crumpled, and he shook his head.

The next fifty minutes were endless as we sat in the waiting room. My eyes hurt from staring at the clock on the wall. When its big hand reached the twelve, I stood up and said, "It's time."

Uncle Bert took my hand and led me into the ward, where four patients were hooked up to wires and monitors and scary-looking machines. After a second I located Punky, from the cowboy hat and the lunch box at the foot of his bed.

"Punk-Man," whispered Uncle Bert. "Delrita's here."

Punky's eyes fluttered open, and he murmured, "My girl."

My eyes burned, and my mouth wouldn't work. I could do nothing but grab Punky's hand and squeeze.

I don't know when Uncle Bert left and Aunt Queenie came in. I know only that before I was ready, she was telling me we had to go.

"Bye, Punky," I whispered. "I'll be back soon."

He held up his right hand. Through blinding tears, I gave him five.

That afternoon and into the evening, I lived for those ten-minute visits, terrified that each one would be the last.

Once, Punky looked at Uncle Bert and said, "My home."

"Soon, Punk-Man, soon."

We stayed at the hospital all night, camping out in the waiting room with borrowed blankets.

Dr. Howe awakened us at dawn. "Mr. Holloway," he said, "there's no change. Your brother's heart is so damaged there's nothing we can do but wait. It defies my medical knowledge why he is still hanging on."

Uncle Bert, looking washed-out and old without his toupee, buried his face in his hands and cried. Aunt Queenie comforted him while I pulled fuzzies off the blanket.

Aunt Queenie went home that day and returned with clean clothes and toiletries for Uncle Bert and me. Neither of us wanted to take the chance of leaving the hospital and coming back to find Punky . . . gone.

We bought a box of crayons in the hospital gift shop. When we next went to see Punky, Uncle Bert sat down and rested his arms on the bed. "Punk-Man," he said, "we brought you something."

Punky opened one eye to look at the crayons and pointed to his lunch box. My heart ached as I slipped the crayons inside, knowing they'd never be peeled and broken.

"Home," whispered Punky. "My home."

"Not yet, Punk-Man," replied Uncle Bert in a strangled voice.

"Bald-head," said Punky, still getting the last word.

The next day, Dr. Howe told us he was moving Punky out of Intensive Care.

"But why?" asked Aunt Queenie. "He's still the same."

Dr. Howe's ears turned red. "That's right, but we're not able to do anything except keep him comfortable—make his breathing easier with that machine. That can be done in another part of the hospital."

At that moment, the ward door whooshed open, and a large nurse bustled out behind a cart, her fat thighs in nylons swishing against each other.

From the ward came a faint cry, "My box. Hands off."

Punky's belongings were on the cart. I bolted from my seat and said, "Wait!"

The nurse just looked at me and moved the cart to make room for Punky, who was being wheeled through.

"Wait," I said again, plucking the cowboy hat and the lunch box off the cart.

The nurse snatched them back and said huffily, "I'm just moving them to another room."

Punky was trying to raise himself up off the bed.

"Young man," said the nurse, "you lie still. You'll fall."

I grabbed the hat and plopped it on Punky's head, but the nurse held tight to the lunch box.

Punky reached for it, and the nurse pulled it back.

"My box," said Punky.

"Miss Hawkins, what's going on here?" asked Dr. Howe.

"I'm just trying to transfer Mr. Holloway to a different room."

"Give him the lunch box."

Reluctantly, Miss Hawkins laid it on Punky's bed.

"You're fat," said Punky, nestling the box under his arm as he was wheeled away.

"Dr. Howe," said Aunt Queenie, "we want to take him home."

"I beg your pardon?"

"You're giving Punky medicine and oxygen when he needs it, and that's all, right?"

"Yes."

"Can't we do the same thing at home?"

"I suppose, but—"

"But what?" asked Aunt Queenie.

"It may be two days. It may be two weeks. But Punky's going to die. Are you prepared to deal with that?"

With tears in her eyes, Aunt Queenie looked at Uncle Bert and then at me. "Yes," she said softly, "we're taking Punky home, where he belongs."

TWENTY-FOUR

Home

Aunt Queenie left the hospital to rent the necessary equipment. A few hours later, Uncle Bert and I went home with Punky.

I looked at the house with new eyes, so very thankful that Punky was here to see it. Christmas lights twinkled in the window, and when Aunt Queenie came out rolling a wheelchair, carols wafted through the door.

I was overwhelmed when I saw what she had done to the family room. Except for the couch, the television set, and the Christmas tree, everything had been moved out to make room for a hospital bed, oxygen equipment, and Punky's punching-bag clown. His clown posters plastered the walls.

Aunt Queenie smiled at me as she helped Punky into bed, saying, "It's good to have everybody home."

Punky was never alone. At night, Aunt Queenie and Uncle Bert took turns sleeping on the couch, and at least one of us sat with him throughout the day.

Not even Mom could have cared for Punky better than Aunt Queenie. She gave him oxygen, washed him, shaved him, fed him when he was too weak to lift a spoon.

I had to go back to school, but my heart was never far away from the family room. Every afternoon, as soon as the last bell rang, I raced out of the building and home.

Home. The word turned over and over in my mind. Punky and I no longer had Mom and Dad, but at last we had a home.

There were days when Punky did nothing but sleep, and others when he wanted his bed cranked up so he could watch TV. I lived for the chance to switch channels for him.

Boss called often, and one afternoon he brought Barney and Susie over for a visit. It broke my heart to see them sitting quietly, their eyes big with anxiety. When it came time for them to go, Susie kissed Punky's cheek and asked, "You come back to work?" Barney gave him five and said, "You're my fwiend."

I tried to carve on Ronald McDonald, but often I'd catch myself just sitting there with the little clown in my hand and my thoughts a million miles away.

When Punky's waking hours became shorter, I forced myself to keep carving so Ronald would be finished in time for Christmas. Deep down, though, I feared Punky wouldn't live that long. Uncle Bert and Aunt Queenie feared it, too. Sometimes in the night, when I couldn't sleep, I'd go to the family room and find them both keeping watch over Punky.

Early one evening, Aunt Queenie seemed to be waiting for something. She kept watching the clock and looking out the window. When footsteps sounded on the porch, she jumped up and ran to the door before the visitor could knock. In a second she was back, and I did a double-take. Behind her were Boss and . . . Santa Claus.

"Ho, ho, ho!" Santa said, winking at me, and I realized he was the general. "Merry Christmas!"

Punky's eyes flew open. "Santy Claus!"

"That's right, my boy, and I've got lots of presents for you in my pack."

Uncle Bert and I helped Punky unwrap his gifts—a T-shirt emblazoned with the American flag, socks, crayons, a wind-up clown, a silly pencil with a fuzzy head on one end, and a soft yellow blanket decorated with figures of Jellybean the Clown.

Tears scalded my throat, and I looked at Aunt Queenie, wondering when she'd had time to do any shopping. Her face was wet. Boss, Uncle Bert, and Santa were crying, too.

Only Punky was happy, and his face practically lit up the room. Within five minutes after Santa and Boss left, he was sound asleep, wearing his new shirt and socks and cuddled in his new blanket.

Aunt Queenie turned down the lights and sat watching TV with Uncle Bert. I sat cross-legged on the tarp on the floor, adding the finishing touches to Ronald with the V-tool, then sanding him and painting him in bright acrylic colors. Bedtime came, but I stayed in the family room. With my family, I thought, as a warmth I hadn't felt for a long, long time enveloped me.

Suddenly Punky sat straight up in bed and pointed at a darkened corner of the room. "Look!" he said. We looked and saw nothing.

"What is it?" asked Uncle Bert in alarm.

"Shirley and Sam. Come home," replied Punky, smiling. He lay down and went back to sleep.

Punky died that night. I held him in my arms and prayed that God would give him back, but it was not to be. The last thing I remember was Aunt Queenie hugging me and saying, "Punky's not handicapped anymore. Now he's like everybody else."

TWENTY-FIVE

Flying

I cried until there was nothing left but a searing pain in my throat and chest. I felt empty and lost and unattached, as if I were floating in the blackness of space, where the lack of gravity would keep me bobbing uselessly forever.

I knew Punky was with Mom and Dad in heaven, but he had left a hole in my life that nothing in the world could fill.

The next morning, Aunt Queenie came to my room and asked gently, "Delrita, honey, can I get you anything?"

"Yes," I said, crawling out of bed to plead with her. "You can get Uncle Bert to have a private funeral. No outsiders. Nobody but family."

"But—"

"Please, Aunt Queenie, please." I couldn't bear to have people laughing and talking around Punky like they had with Mom and Dad. I couldn't bear to think of anyone gawking at him one last time.

Aunt Queenie pushed my bangs off my forehead and gazed into my eyes. "I'll see what I can do," she said. "Now, why don't you take a hot shower?"

After the shower, I hid my shampoo in the drawer before it hit me that I'd never have to hide it again. I wandered into Punky's room and sank down at the sawed-off table where he had spent so many happy hours.

Under the TV, curled up in the dust, was a crayon wrapper. On impulse, I checked behind the set and found three horn bones. They were precious jewels, a reminder that no one, ever, would fling horns as well as Punky. I dug them out and took them to my room.

On the day of the funeral, I sat on my bed with my coat on, wondering how I'd make it through the next couple of hours . . . and the rest of my life . . . without Punky.

From the other part of the house came the muffled sound of voices. Uncle Bert had agreed to a private service, but there were still plenty of relatives on hand. Once again, I had become a blank wall, only vaguely aware of what they were saying: "What a shame . . . Only thirty-five years old . . . He had a happy life. . . . The Lord called him home just when he was beginning to spread his wings. . . ."

"Delrita," said Uncle Bert from the doorway, "we're ready to go."

Numbly, I dropped Ronald McDonald into my

coat pocket and went to slip my hand in Uncle Bert's.

During the service, I pretended I was somewhere else. I stared at the floor, my feet, the back of a chair, anything to avoid seeing the place where Punky lay.

Later, as we rode to the cemetery, Aunt Queenie murmured, "So many flowers. Did you ever see so many flowers?"

Uncle Bert said no and blew his nose, while I stared at my hands in my lap, thinking how the roar of the wind was like a waterfall.

When we reached the cemetery, I hunkered down inside my coat, clutching Ronald McDonald in my pocket as I plodded toward Punky's final resting place. Mom and Dad had been buried here in the early fall, when the grass was still green and birds swooped and chirped nearby. Somehow it seemed more appropriate to see dead grass and to hear nothing but the wailing of the wind.

"Well, I declare," said Aunt Queenie, stopping so fast that I bumped into her.

I glanced up and was shocked to see the gravesite hidden by a mountain of flowers. But Aunt Queenie was looking in the opposite direction. I turned and caught my breath at the sight of a parade.

It looked as though half the town had come to pay tribute to Punky. In the lead were the Veterans of Foreign Wars bearing the American flag. Behind them came Boss, escorting Rudy, followed by the other employees from the sheltered workshop and members of our church. Hot tears sprang to my eyes when I saw Miss Myrtle Chambers, who might have toppled over if it hadn't been for Brother Hicks's wife and Mrs. Shackleford steadying her. Marcus Gregory let go of his mother's hand to wave shyly at me. There were even strangers I had never seen before, and I realized with a start that they somehow must have crossed paths with Punky at the workshop.

I choked back a sob when Coach and the football team marched by in formation, followed by Tree and Avanelle struggling to hang on to a banner that flapped and cracked in the wind. The tears boiled out as I read the words on the banner: "We'll miss you, you old goat."

The people huddled around the grave as if sheltering Punky from the wind, and Brother Hicks began reading from the Bible. Still clutching the little clown in my pocket, I stared at the solemn faces of the crowd. Was it possible that they had all loved Punky, too?

Susie and Barney and Rudy hadn't known him very long, but they were crying. So was Avanelle. And did Tree have dirt in his eye, or was he brushing tears away?

I was squeezing the little clown so hard that a cramp shot up my arm and electrified me with a revelation. Punky had built a fortune in friends, and until this minute, I hadn't seen it. I thought of Whittlin'

Walt's advice about using life wisely to carve out a niche for ourselves.

Punky had used his time wisely. While I had been learning to carve beautiful things with my hands, he had been carving a beautiful niche for himself with his heart.

My fingers holding Ronald McDonald tingled, and I took it as a message from Punky, telling me what to do with the carving.

". . . In Jesus' name we pray. Amen," said Brother Hicks.

"Bang!" I whispered, and gave my body a shake as I felt my invisible shell sliding away. I walked over to Rudy and passed on a tiny part of Punky's happy-go-lucky spirit by placing the clown in his hand. "For you," I said. "It's Ronald McDonald."

Running his fingers over the carving, Rudy questioned me with eyes that couldn't see.

"Because you're a man who loves clowns," I said softly, remembering that Walt had said those same words to Punky at Silver Dollar City.

Tree and Avanelle were near Punky's grave, driving the sticks of their banner into the ground. I hurried over to them, and as they straightened up, I opened my arms and laid them across their shoulders. The gesture reminded me of Herkimer's outstretched wings, and I smiled a secret smile.

"I'm sorry, Delrita," murmured Avanelle, sliding her arm around my waist.

"We'll all miss him," said Tree, as he, too, joined in on the hug.

I closed my eyes and breathed a silent "Thank you" to Punky. No more hiding from the world. No more pretending to be something I wasn't. From now on, I would be myself. Punky had shown me how to make friends, how to be free, and I was going to spread my wings and fly.